To Sheila
and Tony,
Thank you for
listening to me.
Enjoy!
Gisela

Gisela Huberman

LOVE SONGS
for the
DEAD

LAREDO PUBLISHING CO.
BEVERLY HILLS, CALIFORNIA

Published by
Laredo Publishing Co. Inc.
8907 Wilshire Blvd., Beverly Hills, California 90211

This novel is a work of fiction. Names, characters, places, and incidents are
either the product of the author's imagination or are used fictitiously. Any
resemblance to actual persons, living or dead, events or locales is entirely coinci-
dental.

Library of Congress Cataloging In Publication Data

Huberman, Gisela B. 1943-
    Love Songs for the Dead/Gisela Huberman
    p. cm.
    ISBN 1-56492-285-5
    I. Title

PS3558.U239 L68 2000

823'.914--dc21   99-048638

Dedicated

To Leon, my guiding light.
To Pola, my Rock of Gibraltar.
To Ben, my love, my friend, my inspiration.

PROLOGUE

The pain in his leg is unbearable. It's throbbing more than ever. It ruined his plans for today, and it's ruining his life. He's going to have to do something about it very soon.

He limps to the middle of the room, his shoe screeching lightly along the marble floor as he drags his leg forward. When he finally reaches the desk chair, he pitches his body into it with a moan. The stuffed leather chair groans softly as his frame crushes the seat. He lets his arms settle heavily on the mahogany armrests. The veins in his hands bulge as if ready to burst.

He wraps his fingers around his antique pipe and slowly, deliberately, fills it with tobacco blended especially for him. He tamps down the tobacco and gropes for the lighter on the desk. His hand trembles with the effort of sliding the heavy gold lighter toward him over the desktop. The flame is shaky as he holds it to the pipe's bowl and sucks it into the tobacco. Smoke fills the room with the woody aroma that he always enjoys. It smells as though he has stepped into a meadow, early in the morning, just before the hunt. He inhales deeply, smiles, and closes his eyes.

He's all alone now; there's no one else at home. It's quiet here, peaceful. He wishes he weren't feeling so drowsy. He was thinking he would get some work done. He tries to remember whether he's taken more pain killer than usual. But it's hard for him to concentrate. Was he given more than his usual dose? He feels slightly dizzy and tries to massage his forehead, but his arm feels too heavy to lift that high.

Slowly, very slowly, he reaches for a file folder of business letters. He opens it clumsily and turns over its contents one page at a time, pausing between each effort to gather energy for the next. Then he stops, looks over at the fireplace and smiles.

It won't be hard to abandon this way of life. What awaits him is so much sweeter. So much more meaningful. He just hopes he won't hurt too many people by his decision.

He puffs at his pipe, letting the smoke envelop his face. He closes his eyes. And he smiles.

A small rustle out in the hallway distracts him. He opens his eyes and listens. Someone must have left a window open; there's a draft in the room. Odd. The staff know they need to keep the house dry, and it's very damp outside. He tries to get up but stumbles back into his seat.

The whisper of soft footsteps echoes in the distance. He closes his eyes again and leans his head back on the chair. His shirt is choking him. Very slowly, with great effort, he lifts his hand and touches the knot of his tie. He feels for the edges of the knot and pulls at it. Fumbles with it. Finally it gives way and a mother of pearl button rolls down to the floor and he sighs.

There's someone here. He can sense it. He can't see well, can't focus. But, by God he can feel a presence. "Who is it? Who's there?" he calls.

He jerks back. He can see a long, thin sliver of metal coming close to him. It gets closer. He tries to push it back. *My God, what's happening?* He musters all his strength to fend off the attack. A scream, a cry, a show of force. Something.

But only soft mumblings escape his lips. "What do you want? Keep away from me. No! No! Don't!. . . Please!. . . Why?"

His hand flutters to quell the searing spasm in his chest. Then, darkness.

The only sounds in the room are the crackling of the logs in the fireplace and the faint splat of blood drops forming a puddle on the cold marble floor.

1

"I know you're alone and I want you." *My God, it's that same gruff voice again.* It's been three weeks since I heard from him. I thought he was gone for good. And now he's back. *I'll be damned if I show him he scares me.*

"Sir, good evening. Do you have a request?"

"Listen to me, little girl, I've been following your movements for a long time now, don't you dare try to shut me off."

I've got to go on with my shift. The Billy Joel CD is almost over and I need to be back on the air in a few seconds. The last time I hung up on this caller he rang me on my studio phone line every five minutes. It was really unnerving. I've got to be careful with the way I handle him.

"Sir, if you will please hold on, I need to go on the air in a few seconds but then I will come back to talk to you."

"You think I don't know your tricks, little girl? I'm warning you, do not put me on hold because. . ."

"Welcome back. This is WVVV, your love songs radio station. I hope you enjoyed our fifteen-in-a-row, music fans. Please stay tuned. I'll be back after this brief commercial message with some more of your favorite tunes of the fifties, sixties and seventies. This is Gloria Berk, your drive-time deejay." I hope the caller is no longer on the line. I'm feeling a little nervous in this tiny studio, even though it's all glass. But the view of Washington is outstanding. I take a deep breath and start to relax in my modern, comfortable deejay chair. I turn the mike down and go back to the phone:

"Sir . . ." The line is dead. Good. He's gone.

My shift finishes at six, when most of my co-workers at the station have left for the day. Sometimes Sue Hamilton, the general manager, is still working in her office at the opposite end of the studio. On my way out I usually stop by her office, just to chat, to find out the rumors of the day. Mostly I do it just to feel less alone. I still haven't said anything to Sue about my persistent caller. He has called a half dozen times and it's starting to make me uneasy. He's becoming bolder and angrier with each call. It's ridiculous to keep it from Sue but I don't want to complain about something every deejay probably has to put up with at one time or another. Sue seems to have such great control of herself. I don't ever want her to see me cowering or nervous or as someone who doesn't know how to take care of herself. It's really just a matter of pride. I've always looked out for myself. My shift tonight was good. Some shifts are better than others and the shift this evening was better than most. I was witty and warm, I didn't miss a single cue, all the commercials were inserted in good order. I was good. If that fan hadn't called and made me lose my cool for a minute or two, I could even say I had an almost perfect shift.

The lights in the station are still on, but somehow there's an eerie quiet around me. Manny Miranda, the deejay whose program follows mine, is usually around somewhere, but tonight I don't see him. There's usually a straggler or two in the sales office or someone using the phone somewhere. But not tonight. I broadcast the syndicated tape of the six o'clock news and start to walk out through the front door. Management has encouraged us to exit through the back door. It is safer because no one can use it to come in, just to exit, but I think everyone prefers the front door. It's much closer to the elevator.

Sue is gone too. Her office is locked. Just before I reach the front door I hear faint sounds coming out of the staff lounge, just to the left at the end of the hallway. I turn around and walk quietly toward the lounge. I'm standing at the corner of the hallway, not wanting to intrude, but prepared to help if necessary. I hear the muffled voice of a woman starting to rise in volume:

"You don't know what you're doing, you're going to be sorry about this. I promise you. You'll to regret it. Don't you forget it. I'm warning you."

Suddenly Manny comes out of the lounge. He's flustered, excited. He rushes past me without even seeing me standing by the wall, eavesdropping.

"Manny," I call out to him.

"Oh Gloria. I didn't notice you. Sorry. I'm late. My shift is about to begin."

"Manny, what was that all about?"

He shrugs, waves his hand in the air in a dismissive gesture and gently lets himself into the studio. I'm still standing in the hallway, leaning against the pearl-gray wall, staring at the door that just closed. I can see his slim figure dressed all in black through the thick soundproof windows of the studio. Manny is such a good-looking man. Dark hair and eyes, long lean body, sweet smile. Nobody escapes his charm and easy manner. Not a woman. Not a man. His shift starts a few moments after six, so I'm almost never around to see him when he arrives or when his shift is over at midnight. His shift is the time for song dedications. People call in asking for songs to be played to a loved one. To propose. To apologize. And Manny, in his sexy, gentle, playful manner peppers his show with love songs and poems, and bittersweet conversations about lost loves. His voice is perfect for that hour. It lulls, it caresses, it sounds like honey and love-promises. It melts my heart when I hear it. And I never have the chance to just sit and talk with him and admire him.

Whoever was in the lounge with Manny is still there. I walk over and look in. Irma Halifax, the station owner's wife, is standing by the coffee machine and pouring herself a cup of what I know is bitter, day-old coffee.

"Mrs. Halifax, I didn't know you were here."

"No reason for you to know," she snaps back.

She straightens her white cashmere sweater, pushes the long sleeves up, picks up her coffee cup, barely glances in my direction and stalks out of the lounge. When she walks past me I catch a whiff of a most extraordinary fragrance. A mixture of flowers and lemons. Extraordinary. Her bracelets jangle and her blond hair bounces as she walks. She is a most attractive woman.

I glance at my watch. It's six-fifteen. If I don't rush I'll be late for my Criminal Law class. I wrap my blue wool scarf around my neck and run to the front door. As I'm about to open it, three girls, probably in their late teens, push the heavy wooden door open, giggling.

"Hi, where's Manny?"

"Can we see him now?"

"He's in the studio," I answer. "But he's on the air right now. He shouldn't be disturbed."

"Oh, don't worry about it. He invited us here. A lot of our friends have been here. They say it's a lot of fun. He said we could answer some of the phone calls. Omigosh. That's so exciting. Which way to the studio?" I point. "Thank you, oh, hurry up, girls."

I walk out of the station and there's Irma Halifax standing in the hallway waiting for the elevator. She's tapping one foot and looking at her watch. I hesitate, not knowing whether she would like me to ride with her. She turns and looks at me.

"Well, are you coming or not?" she asks impatiently.

I walk faster, get into the elevator after her, and we ride down to the underground garage in silence. I'm relieved I'm not alone. I welcome her company, even if it's silent. We walk out into an almost empty garage, her high heels clacking on the cement floor.

"Do you want me to walk you to your car, Mrs. Halifax?"

"That won't be necessary. It's parked right here, close to

the entrance. Thanks anyway." She walks to a gold Mercedes Benz. It still has temporary tags. Very nice.

My car is parked on the far wall of the garage. I walk very quickly toward it. The garage is well-illuminated, but I notice, for the first time, many recesses where somebody could hide. I climb into my little blue Escort. There's no security guard in the garage. As soon as I get in, I lock the doors and start the motor. Irma's car has long since left the garage. I get to the automatic door and quickly insert my card. The door slides up and finally I'm out in the street, moving.

I'm already late for my class at the law school. I try to rush through the streets of Washington, weaving in and out of very heavy traffic. Wisconsin Avenue is very slow, bumper to bumper. The radio is on, tuned to WVVV, my station, of course. Manny's voice comes on:

"And now, the next selection is dedicated to Rebecca, with love forever and ever from Johnny. That's right, Johnny, always tell 'em how much you love 'em. Let's listen now to 'Unforgettable,' out of the lovely lips of Miss Natalie Cole. This is Manny the Silver Fox, your messenger of love."

What a voice! What a magnificent, caressing voice. My pulse quickens when I hear that glorious voice.

The class has already started. I sneak in, hoping that my professor won't notice I'm late. But he does. The doors to the classroom creak when you open them, no matter how slowly or carefully you do it. He looks up and sees me walking in, stepping on other people's toes, trying to get to an empty seat in the last row. He smiles. I smile back. Peter Wilson. My

Criminal Law professor. I'm not sure whether I like the class so much because I find the topic fascinating or because Peter is so charismatic and kind-hearted, the best professor I have ever had. It doesn't hurt that I find him so attractive. His sparkling wide smile and deep blue eyes hypnotize me. I look forward to my class, Mondays and Thursdays and study hard to prepare for them. I choose carefully what I'm going to wear those days. However, I don't think Peter has noticed me much. My plan is that if I do well in this class and can start saving a little money, who knows, I might be able to go to law school at night, instead of just this extension course. I'll get my degree in law and expand my horizons. My parents would certainly like that.

As the class ends, I collect my books very slowly, trying to extend my time in Peter's presence. I glance down at the podium once in a while, to see if he's about to leave. I'd like to walk out with him, to have a few seconds of his attention devoted entirely to me. As always, he's surrounded by other students. Slowly, very slowly I put on my navy blue jacket and tie my blue scarf around my neck. He has not glanced in my direction even once. I walk out of the classroom. At the doorway, I feel a hand on my shoulder.

"Gloria, would you like some coffee?"

It's Steve, a young policeman who was sitting next to me in class. He must have been waiting for me outside the auditorium. I smile. "Not tonight, Steve. Sorry, I have to prepare for tomorrow's show. Maybe next time." This is not Steve's first invitation. We went to have coffee last week. Nice guy. Eager guy. Too eager. For a woman's body. It was very hard to keep him from groping my breasts.

The student parking lot seems far off now. I'm striding fast, to reach the gate. I'm walking alone. It's very dark and the traffic is sparse. My law books are under my arm and, as usual when I walk at night, my car key is sticking out between my index and third fingers. The only weapon I can come up with.

I hear footsteps behind me. I accelerate my pace. I'm too nervous to turn around. There are very few cars left in the parking lot at this hour and there's no guard. The footsteps are getting closer. I don't know if I should run or stop. Finally, I can't stand the suspense and I spin around suddenly to face my pursuer. *Oh, my God. It's Mr. Wilson.* Peter is standing in front of me.

"Ms. Berk, are you parked in this lot? I saw you walking alone and I thought I'd walk you to your car. We've had a few ugly incidents around here lately. I hope I didn't startle you."

I can hardly breathe. "Oh no, no, Mr. Wilson, of course you didn't startle me. Please call me Gloria. Is your car parked here too?"

"Call me Peter. I didn't drive tonight. I'm taking the Metro. I was crossing over to Tenley Park to the Metro station. It's just a few blocks from here. Forgive me if I startled you."

I must look like a ghost. "Of course not, Mr. Wilson. I'm perfectly all right. Can I give you a lift? My car is right here." *Please, please let him say yes. Let him spend just a few more minutes with me.*

"If it doesn't take you out of your way."

Thank you, God. What did I do to deserve this? "Of course not, it's my pleasure."

We both get into my little car. I'm so happy and excited I can hardly insert the key in the ignition. We start to pull out of the lot. Suddenly a car coming from Wisconsin Avenue careens straight toward us. It almost hits us in front. I stop as fast as I can, and we lurch forward. I reach for Peter's hand "Are you all right?" He nods yes.

I look straight at the driver of the other car. It's Steve. He stares at me and Peter and drives away.

"Do you want me to drive?" Peter asks.

"No, thanks. I'm all right." I'm not all right, I'm shaking all over.

"Would you care to stop for a few minutes and have some coffee?"

"I'd love to."

We're sitting at Mama Aliya's Café. It's almost empty. Some oriental music is playing in the background. The café smells of a mixture of cardamon, ginger, and other exciting spices. Quite intoxicating.

I order a strong Turkish coffee. I'm sure I'm going to be up all night anyway thinking about the incident with Steve and the silly calls I've been getting. Plus my coffee date with Peter. So it doesn't make a difference how strong the coffee is. Peter asks for a beer. We talk for a while about class, about the students there, and about my job.

"Have you ever heard my show?".

"I don't listen to radio much." he answers. "Maybe only when I'm driving to work sometimes."

"Well, now that you have a radio personality in your class,

you'll have to listen to me. I would really like your opinion."

"I'll listen whenever I have a chance."

"Promise?"

"Promise!"

"You know, it's really great sitting here with you like this. Talking, I mean. Relaxing. I'm enjoying this very much."

"Well, then, we'll just have to do this more often." He smiles, just barely touching my fingertips.

We've reached the Metro station. I don't want Peter to leave yet. But I don't know how to keep him with me any longer.

"Well, kiddo, this was fine. Just fine." He reaches for my hand and lightly presses his lips to my fingers. It makes me shiver. "I'll see you in class on Thursday. Study hard." He gets out of the car, turns to me and smiles. I don't move the car until he disappears into the shadows of the darkened subway station.

I run up the steps to my third floor walk-up two steps at a time. I'm floating. I fling open the door and skip inside. The amber light of my answering machine is flashing, bathing the small apartment in an iridescent glow. I dance over to turn it on to hear the messages:

"I know where you live and I know what you're doing. Don't reject me ever again." *Oh God! Could it be Steve?*

2

I've never seen a house quite like this one. I've been invited to a cocktail party at the Halifax estate, the home of the station's owner on the outskirts of Washington. Some of the station's staff occasionally get invited. This is the first time I've been asked to attend. So, even though my day at the station was uneventful, I couldn't get my mind off tonight's affair. Mr. Halifax's cocktail parties are famous all over the city. Many Washington politicians and artists put in appearances.

I park my little blue Ford Escort in a small space between two larger cars in the circular brick driveway. I read somewhere, *Washingtonian Magazine*, I think, that Mr. Halifax imported these bricks from his native England. I walked toward the grand pillared entrance. Impressive stone columns support a very high roof over a slate porch.

A butler welcomes me at the doorway with a tray of champagne glasses. The stained-glass doors open onto a cavernous two-story reception hall. My entire apartment could easily fit into this foyer.

As soon as I step in, I'm engulfed by works of art. I'm completely surrounded by beautiful art objects and paintings. A Chihuly chandelier hangs in the entryway. There's a genuine Gauguin over the mantelpiece, an authentic Picasso over the piano. I'm astounded. I've seen pieces of this quality only in museums. Never in a private collection. The women around me look spectacular. They're wearing long glittering gowns and beautiful jewels. I'm curious, I'd like to go and explore the whole house, see how Mr. Halifax lives and how Irma lives. But apparently everybody is supposed to stand around the grand piano in the living room at the left of the entrance hall. It is a black Steinway. A young man with long dark blond hair in a pony tail and a frayed tux is playing Gershwin. Nobody's paying any attention to him. I recognize a Chihuly aqua blue glass sculpture on the piano. It's one of his famous Seaforms. Beautiful. I saw a piece similar to this one at the Renwick Gallery just last week.

Irma is standing in the middle of the living room surrounded by six or seven men. She's certainly the most glamorous of all the women here. She's wearing a long white strapless silk dress that emphasizes her round full breasts. It's slit on one side to reveal a glimpse of her gorgeous leg every time she takes a step. Her blond hair, cut to her shoulders and combed to one side, glistens. Her diamond and sapphire earrings sparkle every time she tosses her head as she laughs. It's a throaty, sexy laugh. Her arm is intertwined with the arm of a good-looking tall man while one foot is playfully kicking another man's shin. I can't keep my eyes off her. She certainly doesn't notice me at all.

Someone taps me softly on the shoulder. "Hi stranger, is it glamorous enough for you?" It's Sue, our general manager. She's wearing a long black velvet skirt with a loosely fitting gold sequined top. She's tall, slim, and elegant.

"Sue, this is great." I am genuinely happy to see her. "What a place. Why am I here? How come I was invited?"

"Nothing strange about that. Mr Halifax likes to have his people over from time to time. Share the art and the drinks, I suppose." She smiles. " We wanted you to have a good time."

"We?" I ask "Who is we?"

"Oh, Mr. Halifax and I. We both thought it would be a good idea for you to be seen out in public. We want the world to know our disc jockeys. Besides, Mr. Halifax wants to talk to you."

Oh my God. I'm in trouble. What did I do now? Mr. Halifax, the owner of the station does not talk to lowly employees like me. He has his general managers do the talking for him. "To me?" I ask quietly. "Did I do something wrong?"

"No, silly. He'd just like to say a few words to you. Follow me. He's waiting for you in his den."

I smooth my short black dress, the best thing I own, and catch a glimpse of myself in a mirror in the hallway. My short auburn hair looks decent enough, my eye make-up isn't smudged. I guess it will have to do for the first meeting with our elusive owner.

I follow Sue down the long hallway. There is art hanging

on every wall, but I can't concentrate on what I am looking at. I'm too nervous. The noise of the party is becoming less audible. I try to minimize the clacking my high heels are making on the marble floor by walking almost on tiptoes. We walk past various rooms with open doors and I try to peer in to satisfy my curiosity. At a glance, I see antiques, brightly lit chandeliers, and art everywhere. It is an incredible house. My mind, however, is reeling. *What could Mr. Halifax want with me?* Sue smiles. "Nice little place he's got here, huh?" she says.

"I'll say."

We finally reach a closed door. Sue knocks gently, almost hesitantly on the mahogany doors. An English-accented voice says, "It's open."

My God, he sounds just like James Mason. We walk into a surprisingly simple dark paneled office. There's a glass-top desk, a small blue oriental rug on the white marble floor. The walls are lined with mahogany bookshelves, fully stocked with books. In the far corner, close to the fireplace, Mr. Halifax is just turning to greet us. I notice a rack with a large collection of guns on the wall behind him. Here and there are gorgeous glass sculptures, which lift the atmosphere of the room, making it cheerful, light-hearted, playful.

I like Mr. Halifax immediately. What a handsome face. He's smoking a pipe, and the smoke encircles his sparse gray hair. He has a strong chin and a square jaw. His smiling blue eyes turn to us and sparkle invitingly.

As he walks toward me, leaning on a carved ebony cane, his right hand is extended in a warm welcome. His navy blue blazer shows off a lean figure with broad shoulders. I read in a station bio that he's sixty-eight years old, but he looks so much younger.

"Sit down, my dear, won't you please," he says, pointing to a brown leather couch. It's very soft leather. "Thank you, Sue. I'll talk to Ms. Berk alone." *I hope I'm not in trouble. I really like this man.*

Sue looks at each of us, hesitates for a second and then closes the door behind her very gently. My stomach takes a tumble. Mr. Halifax sits down next to me. The woody smell of his pipe envelops me.

"I've been listening to your show, Ms. Berk. May I call you Gloria?" He asks.

"Of course, Mr. Halifax, certainly," I say very quickly.

"Thank you. I like your show very much, especially the detective contest you've devised. It's very clever."

My God, he's actually complimenting me. What could come next?

"Thank you very much, Mr. Halifax. Your words mean a lot to me."

"Now, I have a favor to ask of you." He draws a puff on his pipe, looks at me and smiles. "It's a big favor, but I know you won't say no. Will you?"

"Mr. Halifax, I'll do whatever you ask me." *What else can I say?*

"My dear, it's about my wife."

"Oh, Mr. Halifax. She's a very beautiful woman."

"Yes, yes." I think I hear a note of impatience here. "Well, she's been pressing me to put her on the radio. She has nothing to do, she says. Her friends will be impressed by her being

on the air, she says, she'll do whatever we ask of her. I thought
that if you would use her in your "Crime in the Afternoon"
contest, she might be content and stop badgering me and my
general manager. You can give her just a few short lines, in
whatever script you'd like her to read. I know it's an imposi-
tion on you and I do appreciate very much your help here.
Please tell Sue tomorrow the role you've assigned my wife,
won't you?"

So, that's the way an owner asks for a favor.

Mr. Halifax puffs one more time on his pipe, stands up,
and leads me gently by the arm to the door. "Please continue
having a good time, won't you?" he says with a smile. With
that, he opens the door, and I follow the sounds of the party.

Irma is standing in the middle of the living room. The
center of attention. Her arm is caressing Manny's; he looks
uncomfortable, stiff. His eyes are downcast and a plastic smile
is plastered on his face. She doesn't seem to notice his discomfort. She's standing very close to him. Now her breast is
rubbing lightly against his arm. I see it moving from right to
left, from left to right. She looks at me as I make my way
down the hallway to the living room. It's a cold, icy stare. My
smile freezes on my lips.

I'm on the George Washington Parkway, driving very fast
on my way home. I cross the Potomac River and let the memories of my childhood in Potomac transport me for a while. I
grew up in a small house no more than two miles from the
Halifax estate, but in a different world. It was a sweet, quiet,
loving childhood. I turn on the radio and hear Manny's voice:

"To Edwina from Mark: please stay with me. I will love you forever. Yes, Mark, yes. Tell her you love her."

Last week's tape is being replayed.

I climb the three flights to my small apartment. Small but mine. It's a very nice apartment in the middle of Adams Morgan, in the center of Washington, surrounded by coffee shops, quaint boutiques, small ethnic restaurants and many bars. A noisy neighborhood. It's October and the Washington evenings are starting to get cool. I fling open the doors to my small balcony. The sweet smell of some flower wafts into my place. I think it is jasmine. I don't mind the noise outside. It's a happy noise of people laughing and enjoying the evening. Suddenly I'm starving. I had too much champagne at the Halifax party and too little to eat. Just two or three little snacks that were being passed around. Some sort of stuffed mushrooms, I think. And a few pieces of cheese. I need food. Real food! I'm a good cook but I hate to eat alone. And I feel very alone tonight. I think about Peter. I would love to call him but I don't even know where he lives. Or if he's married. I feel hungry and alone.

The phone rings. It's close to eleven.

"Hello." *Peter, I hope it's you.*

"Gloria, Manny here." His voice sounds very subdued. Where is that rich baritone, that melodious, caressing voice that I know and love so well?

"Manny, where are you? What's going on?" He has never called me this late before.

"Can I come see you? I think I'm in trouble." His voice is

very still.

"Sure, Manny, come on over. Do you remember where I live?"

"Of course. It hasn't been that long since I was there." He hangs up .

I go to the kitchen to prepare some eggs, cheese, and potatoes. I turn on the radio. It's still Manny's old show: "And from Paul to Liza: I'll never forget last night."

Ah, that voice. That wonderful voice. It moves my heart. It stirs my loins.

3

My kitchen is really not large enough for two people, so I ask Manny to sit on the small love seat facing the kitchen. I can cook and look at him at the same time.

He looks good sitting there, as if he belongs. His long, lean body dressed all in black–black jeans, black turtleneck, black loafers–contrasts very nicely with the gold-colored sofa. Everything I have here was once in my parents' house. They decided to get all new furniture when they moved to Boca Raton. Something "fresh and light; something very Florida," as my mother put it. They gave me whatever I could use. So my apartment looks well decorated.

I'm cooking for Manny and me. I turned off the radio and put on my CD changer filled with classical music CD's. Mozart's Jupiter Symphony is on. Whenever I listen to CDs at home, I choose classical music. I was raised on it. My father plays the violin and my mother plays the piano. For years I tried to play a decent tune on the piano and never could move past "Fur Elise"–kids' stuff. So now I just listen to CD's.

It's good to have Manny in my apartment. Gorgeous Manny with the soulful dark eyes and the full mouth. The balcony doors are still open, but it's late now, after midnight, and the noise in the street has died down considerably. Soaring Mozart is still on. And the scent of the flowers outside gets stronger as night falls. I must identify that flower. I love it so.

Manny is very pale, his long dark hair disheveled. His eyes are unfocused. His lips are slightly parted. "Gloria, do you mind if I smoke? I really need a smoke."

"Go ahead." I search for something that resembles an ash tray. I find a candy dish; my mother said it was cut glass from Poland. I don't use it at all as I never buy any candy. And what better use for it than for Manny's cigarette butts? I like everything about Manny. I hand him the candy dish and his fingers touch my hand. Cool, long fingers. They give me a jolt. He puffs quietly as I go on cooking. The apartment is very quiet except for Mozart's music.

I'm preparing my signature dish–cheese and potatoes omelette, with a mound of fried plantains on the side. It's a mouth-watering combination. My mother's own invention, influenced by some Cuban friends, I think. The aroma of the eggs and the jasmine-like flowers outside the window is intoxicating. Mozart has given way to a Beethoven piano sonata. Manny is immersed in his own thoughts. He's very quiet. I wish he would just sit there, not discuss any problems with me. Just let me look at him sitting in my apartment and let me daydream about him.

He looks at me. I think this is the first time since we've known each other that he's really looked at me. Ever. I feel myself blush down to my neck. I smile at him. I want these seconds to last a long, long time.

"Mr. Halifax wants me out," he says, letting out a long sigh. "My entire career, all my dreams, everything I've worked for is going down the drain, Gloria. I don't know what to do. It's going to kill my parents. They're so proud of me, of my accomplishments. I'm the first person in the entire family who's broken away from being a servant. The first one who's gone to college. And here I am, facing ruin, embarrassment and a law suit." He puts his head between his hands and lets out a muffled sob. "Mr. Halifax said he would make sure I'll never find another job in radio. Radio is all I know, it's my life, the only thing I've ever done."

I'm speechless. Manny's such a good disc jockey, a thorough professional, always ready for his show, and he has the greatest following of listeners at the station. He's expecting my reaction.

"Manny, is it because of Irma? I've seen the way she looks at you, the way she makes it a point to come to the station when you're there."

"No, no," he says quickly. Too quickly, I think.

I serve the eggs with the plantains and slices of fresh French bread and open a bottle of white wine. We sit at the small round dining table facing the balcony. I think about lighting a candle, but Manny's mood is too somber. It's not the right moment to appear romantic.

"What happened, Manny? How can I help?"

"I need an attorney. Can you ask your professor at the law school to help me find one? I don't know any lawyers. I wouldn't even know how to get one. Halifax told me the station's going to be sued for millions of dollars because of me." He's hardly touching his food. I feel guilty eating when he's feeling so low.

He lights another cigarette, takes a long puff and lets out the smoke very slowly. I close my eyes and let the smoke penetrate my nostrils.

"They're accusing me of raping a minor, Gloria. A minor. A fifteen-year old girl."

I bolt upright in my chair. "Who's accusing you, Manny? How? I don't understand."

"Sometimes. . ." He's talking very softly now, I need to strain to hear him well. ". . . at night, when I'm all alone in the station, I have visitors. Occasionally men, sometimes women. Mostly women. Some are young women, very young. I never ask their age. We talk, we laugh, sometimes I let them answer my phone calls. They like that a lot. Sometimes we kiss. Sometimes we pet. We may pet heavily on occasion. But I have never, ever had a sexual encounter at the station with anyone. I swear to you Gloria, never. I've never raped anyone in my life. I've never encouraged anyone to come see me. I don't know what I'm going to do."

"What does Halifax have to do with this ?"

"Tonight, at the party, he summoned me to his den." He lights another cigarette. "He told me that the girl's attorney —a guy named Sconix—has threatened a law suit against the radio station. He's also threatening to file a complaint with the Federal Communications Commission about all this. Halifax is afraid that if this goes public his entire radio empire will come under scrutiny. At the very least it will give him bad publicity and he might lose advertisers and the trust of his investors. Sconix told him that they are willing to come to an agreement and settle all this quietly out of court."

"How much?" I ask

"Twenty million dollars."

"My God. Twenty million dollars! What does Halifax want you to do?"

"He told me I have to do whatever it takes to stop this suit. I'm supposed to talk to the girl and apologize and convince her and her mother to drop the suit, to forget about any settlements." He pauses. "I'm supposed to marry the girl if I must, or lose my job."

"Dear God. How can I help you, Manny?"

"Talk to your law professor. Find out what I should do. I didn't rape the girl, Gloria. I swear to you. And I want to keep my job. I love my job. I've worked so hard to get to where I am. It's been my ambition for such a long time. I can't possible let it go." His voice dies down. He looks exhausted.

"Don't worry, Manny. I'll talk to my professor tomorrow. He seems to be very kind. I'm sure he'll help you somehow."

Manny pushes aside his almost untouched plate, gulps down his wine, and slowly stands up to his full six foot-three height. He walks slowly to where I'm sitting, takes my face in his hands, caresses my cheecks and bends down to kiss my forehead. I inhale the aroma of his cologne.

"Good night, Gloria. Thank's for listening to me. For helping. You're a great friend. I'll see you tomorrow at the station." He turns and leaves.

The music is still playing. It's the second movement of Beethoven's Seventh Symphony. How I love the point-counter-point of that melody, its powerful rhythmic tension. It's complex, lyrical, and joyous all at once. I stare out the window to look at Manny. I see his lonely, stooped figure retreating slowly up the deserted street. I pick up the soiled dishes and take them to the kitchen. I can wash them tomorrow. I close the doors to the small balcony. Manny's cologne still lingers in the air.

After a fitful night, I arrive at the station to see Irma waiting for me. My shift is "drive time," from two to six p.m. Irma's dressed in a denim mid-calf skirt, a tight white silk shirt, and red sandals with straps wrapped around her bare tanned ankles. Enormous sunglasses cover her face. Standing at the reception desk, she pushes her glasses to the top of her head. "Come to my office with me," she says. No hello. No greeting of any kind.

Her small office is across the hall from the reception desk. It's not impressive at all. Just a desk, a phone, one chair for her and two guest chairs. Some shelves, no books. Just some pictures of her with Senators and Congressmen. On her desk, facing guests, she's placed a large silver frame with a photo of her smiling broadly at the President standing beside her with an arm around her bare shoulders. Her big brown eyes are sparkling. Sitting at her desk she has a perfect view of everyone who arrives and leaves the station.

She motions for me to sit in one of the guest chairs, while she goes around her desk, takes out a cigarette–even though it's forbidden to smoke anywhere in the building–and without looking at me says: "I've been waiting for you for almost an hour. Where have you been?" She is visibly angry.

"My shift starts in half an hour. . ."

She doesn't let me finish. "My husband said you had a project for me. I'd like to begin right away. I already told my friends and they're waiting to hear me on the radio."

"Irma, Mrs. Halifax, can I call you Irma?"

"Everybody else does. You're no different." Her English is softly accented. Her j's are soft. "Project" sounds like "proyect". Her accent adds to her air of exoticism.

"Irma, I have a new contest called 'Crime in the Afternoon'," I explain. "I'll provide a few clues to the listeners and they'll get prizes for every correct guess. During the final week of the contest we'll pool all the winners and they'll compete to solve 'The Crime of the Century' puzzle. It's going to be more difficult, but the winner will win a brand new Jaguar XK8 convertible. It's an awesome car. Your husband was generous enough to allow me to give away such a great car."

"He's not a generous man. Make no mistake about that," she says. "He's allowing you to give it away only because he knows that it'll bring in a lot of listeners. It's a good contest and it'll get a lot of talk around town. The more people talk about it, the more advertisers we'll attract. That always pleases my husband. How do I fit in?"

"Well, I thought I would make you a detective, perhaps

'Detective Sabrina' or something like that. I'll call you in your office, at the beginning of the contest every day, and you'll provide the first clue of the afternoon."

She's thinking about it, drumming her red fingernails on the desk and puffing away at her cigarette. "I like it," she finally says with a smile–she has beautiful white straight teeth. "I like it. Detective Sabrina fits me just fine. When do we start?"

"Today, if you'd like, at five-fifteen sharp. Will you be ready?"

"Of course. What time does Manny get in?"

"Usually around five-thirty to get ready for his show." I don't like talking about Manny with her. "His show starts right after the 6 o'clock news."

"Well, hurry up and give me my lines. I want to be prepared. And make me sound interesting."

"I'll bring them in while my first song is playing."

It's five-fifteen sharp. I dial Irma's office. "Ladies and gentlemen, let's welcome Detective Sabrina, who will be joining us daily to give us the first clue of the day. Good afternoon, Detective Sabrina,"

"Good afternoon, Gloria." The voice is smooth and purring, warm, sophisticated.

"Can you tell us about today's 'Crime in the Afternoon'?" I'm hoping and praying that everything goes smoothly. It's my contest. I really don't want her to ruin it. And I don't have any choice about keeping her. Her husband wants her in the contest.

"Of course, Gloria. It appears that the great pianist

Mozelli has died leaving an inheritance of forty million dollars to Mozelli's closest relative. The will is probated and two potential inheritors show up. Only one is the real relative. The other is an impostor. Mr. Marius claims he's Mozelli's great nephew. Ms. Lewis claims Mozelli is her grandfather. The executor awards the forty million to Mr. Marius. Why"?

"Thank you, Detective Sabrina."*My God*, I marvel, *she's good. She's very, very good.* "Well, ladies and gentlemen, put on your thinking caps. The first correct caller will win one thousand dollars. If nobody gets it, I'll provide you with the second clue in fifteen minutes. But the prize money will go down to seven hundred and fifty dollars. Good luck and good hunting to all of you!"

Manny's here. I see him walk in heading toward the studio. Irma rushes out of her office. Taking long strides, she catches up to him. She slides an arm through his and pulls him into her office.

The door to her office closes behind them.

4

"We have a winner!" I announce brightly. "Ms. Norma Christopher from Alexandria, Virginia has won one thousand dollars from WVVV for the correct answer! The answer is that the closest relative is the grand nephew, the other is an impostor. Ms. Lewis didn't know that the great Mozelli was a woman. Ms. Lewis identified her as her "grandfather." Congratulations, Ms. Christopher. Your name has been entered into the All Winners' Big Crime Solvers and you may be the lucky winner of a brand new Jaguar convertible. We'll have a new crime puzzle tomorrow afternoon. Keep listening to WVVV for Manny the Silver Fox's program "Love Songs." Goodbye and good hunting. And now the news."

Irma had been unexpectedly good. I am quite surprised.

I take the elevator to the garage, jump in my car and start driving to American University for my criminal law class. I don't want to be late to class again. I need to see Peter. Also, I want to talk to him about Manny.

It's raining. Traffic is worse than ever. It usually takes me fifteen minutes to get to my class. Today I'll be lucky if I'm there by the time class starts at seven.

I turn on the radio to my station. Sometimes I listen to other stations to hear what the competition is doing. Manny's on. He sounds as mellow, as romantic and caressing as ever. "And now, Frank Sinatra singing 'I've Got You Under My Skin', dedicated to Lucy from Robert: Please forgive me for last night, Lucy, it didn't mean a thing; you're my true love. Good luck, Robert, I hope this helps." The same soothing, marvelous voice.

I find a parking space several blocks away. I get out and hike in the rain to my class. I sit down in the back row of the auditorium. Steve is seated two rows in front of me. I really would like to avoid him tonight. I feel a little scared of him. But he turns around when I walk in and when he sees me, he gets up, walks up the two rows and leans over to speak to me.

"I'm so sorry about last time. I was shocked when I saw I almost hit you head on. I almost froze. Please forgive me. I really didn't see you."

I listen intently to his voice. *It's not the voice on the telephone. I don't think it's the same voice.* I put my hand on his, smile at him and assure him "It's all right, Steve. I'm glad nobody got hurt." He squeezes my shoulder and sprints back to his seat.

There are about forty-five students in the class. I think everyone witnessed our exchange. I smile and shrug. Peter is in the middle of an impassioned speech about victims' rights. He stresses that sometimes the law makes mistakes and the wrong person gets arrested. He talks about how careful we must be that all the correct procedures are followed to safeguard the rights of the innocent. He speaks with great force. As always, he's fascinating, a charismatic teacher. I hope he doesn't call on me because I haven't had a chance to prepare for the class. I haven't read any of the assigned cases. I wouldn't know what to answer if he called on me. Whenever he asks a question, I avert my eyes. I have the magical notion that if I don't see him, he won't see me.

At the end of the class I walk down the ten steps to the podium. As always, he's surrounded by students peppering him with questions. Mostly, I hear them questioning his liberal views. He tries to answer each one of them. After a while he notices me standing at the corner of the podium, leaning against the wall. He smiles, and after a few more minutes, he excuses himself from the half-dozen students who are still hanging on and walks over to me. He has a long stride and he looks good in his business suit. The top button of his shirt is unbuttoned and his tie is loose. I notice that some chest hair is peeking from the open shirt. I'm sure I'm smiling broadly when he approaches me.

"You came in late and you weren't prepared for class," he says with a hearty laugh. His blue eyes are merry, his short brown hair disheveled. I notice a strip of moisture on his upper lip. I'm dying to reach over and wipe it with my fingers.

"Sorry, the traffic was murder tonight."

"Sure, it's always the traffic." He smiles again. "Is there

any question I can clarify for you?"

"Peter, I need your help. Actually, it's a guy at my station who needs it. I hope you don't mind, I told him I'd talk to you. I'm sure you'll be able to help him."

" Tell me the details. I'll be glad to help if I can."

"Can I invite you for some coffee?" I offer. "There's a cute coffee bar a block away."

"Actually, I'm starving. I haven't had a chance to eat anything all day. Let's go to Nam Viet. I love Vietnamese food, and they stay open late." *Dinner with Peter! This is absolutely great!*

We meet at the restaurant on Connecticut Avenue, in a neighborhood filled with outdoor cafes. It's only about five minutes from my apartment, in a more upscale, quieter neighborhood. It's cold and late at night so everything seems abandoned. But our little restaurant is warm, surprisingly full of people and quite good. Over a plate of *pho*, delicious broad Vietnamese noodles swimming in a clear delicate broth, I tell him about Manny's plight. He listens attentively. He doesn't interrupt me once or make any comments. Finally, when I finish, he says he'll look into it and call me tomorrow. That's all he says.

I give him my phone number. My *home* phone number. "Thanks," I say.

The staff lounge is crowded. It's a relaxed Friday afternoon, a few minutes before my show starts. I pour myself a cup of disappointing lukewarm coffee–someone turned off the warmer–and Tim Elias, our news director, joins me and kids around with me about the upcoming weekend. "You must have many dates, huh Gloria? How do you choose among the throngs?"

He makes me laugh. I like Tim. He has such a serious air about him, but he's really a wonderful, easy-going colleague. His sense of humor is wry and witty and can go mano-a-mano with the best morning disc jockeys in the business. He doesn't miss a beat. There's no book he hasn't read and no important article he can't discuss with charm and intelligence. People seem to put complete trust in this six-foot-tall, very thin man, with a sweet smile and inquisitive brown eyes. He always dresses in chinos, a white shirt and a bow tie. Always the same.

We sit at the small round table in the lounge, facing each other, and I give him my best imitation of Irma. I borrow one of his cigarettes, hold it as gracefully as I can manage between my second and third fingers, pout my lips and purr: "Dear Gloria." I actually purr, "I looooove being Detective Sabrina. . ." Suddenly Tim's smile freezes, he becomes pale and he manages to point to the door facing him. I turn around in mid-sentence and there she is, in all her glory, Irma in a yellow jumpsuit and black high-heeled sandals. She's staring at me, her hands on her hips and a thin smile across her red lips. She just looks at me and doesn't say a word. Then she turns around and sways her way back to her office. *God, please, just take me this second, I want to die.*

A staff meeting with Arnold Watson, Mr. Halifax's attorney, has been called. We're all required to attend. It's a very strained meeting. All of us at the station, every single one from Veronica the receptionist to Sue the general manager, are crammed into the conference room. It's an elegant room with an enormous window overlooking Wisconsin Avenue. I stare out the window. It's raining again. The leaves are starting to turn to orange and gold. People are hurrying down in the street, carrying big black umbrellas. Our offices and studios are comfortable but not too elegant. Except for the exquisitely appointed reception and conference room areas. But because we are so high up, occupying the entire eighth floor of the building, we have spectacular views of D.C. We hardly ever use the conference room. It's used mostly by Tim Elias, the news director, when he conducts interviews with community leaders for our public affairs programs. Mr. Halifax has used it from time to time to hold business meetings with potential investors. Otherwise the conference room stays empty. Today the room is filled to capacity. I found a seat when I walked in but promptly gave it to Veronica, the receptionist, who's six months pregnant. So I'm standing. The atmosphere is charged. We are all nervous. An all-staff meeting with the owner's attorney is an extremely rare occurrence. We wonder if the station is being sold and if any of us will lose our jobs. Only a few of us, very few, have a contract with the station. The rest are hired "at will," a fancy way to tell us we can be fired for any reason at all. Only the "superstars" have contracts, mainly because the administration is afraid of losing them to other stations. And the superstars, if they left our station, would most likely take their loyal listeners with them. And what is a radio station without an audience.

I don't have a contract. Strangely, neither does Manny,

41

even though I think he's by far the best disc jockey at the entire station. I think only the morning team of Jay and Mark, the ones who make the big bucks are the only ones that have contracts. Therefore, we are all are very, very nervous, except for the stars of "The Jay and Mark Show."

The phones are ringing constantly, and there is no one to answer them. My shift is being covered by a part-time disc jockey, a student who is playing at being a deejay. When I walked into the conference room, I heard him announce that tonight we would have clear skies with the sun shining brightly. Ah, well. I can see my audience dwindling by the minute.

Arnold Watson, of the law firm of Watson, Wilkins, Simmons & Carey, is an impressive man. He's very tall and must weigh over two hundred pounds. A fringe of gray hair frames a reddish face with a bulbous nose and full lips. He marches into the conference room wearing an olive green rumpled suit, a cotton shirt, and a brown tie encrusted with a few spots. Standing at the head of the table, he lays down his briefcase with a loud thud and stares at us. Without preamble, he says in a booming voice: "We're all in a shitload of trouble." The room quiets down immediately.

We look up expectantly and nervously. Suddenly I notice that Manny is absent.

There are a few seconds of silence. Watson takes a sip of coffee. Some drops remain on his upper lip, which he ignores.

"If you want to keep your jobs at this radio station, you will listen very carefully. There will be no more visitors to our studios. Do you get me? No more dalliances with young, innocent, wide-eyed groupies who follow you everywhere."

His thick lips are almost purple as he speaks. They seem to take on a life of their own. "After hours, these doors stay closed. Not one of you, except for your general manager, can invite anyone to come into the radio station after five o'clock. No one. I hope I'm making myself crystal clear. We just hired Lew Jenkins, a retired police officer, to guard the station. He'll be posted outside this station every evening from the time the business office closes until the doors open again at eight a.m. If any one of you disobeys these orders you will be dismissed on the spot. No questions asked. No exceptions made. I will do whatever possible to safeguard Mr. Halifax's investment. The radio station is his investment. All of you are expendable, I'm sure you're aware of that. Mr. Halifax will not lose this radio station because one of you hot shots has ants in your pants and can't wait to get out of here and run to the nearest motel. You follow me, I'm sure. This goes for all you wonderful women in here, too. I hope I'm making myself perfectly clear."

No one says a word. Everyone is transfixed. Sue is pale and looks very uncomfortable. She is standing behind Veronica's chair, swaying from side to side, gripping the back of the chair, her knuckles white, her eyes bloodshot. The rest of us motionless.

In one of the corners of the room, Renata, a young salesperson in her first month with the station, whispers loudly to Tim, standing next to her: "Why is he doing this?"

Watson, who is leafing through some papers, stops dead, looks up, turns to Renata, his face bright red, his lips swollen and purple and exclaims: "My dear young thing, whoever you are. You want to know why I'm doing this?" His small green eyes bore into her. Those eyes make me shiver. "Because one of your esteemed colleagues, the wonderful Manny Miranda, the Silver Fox, as he calls himself, or rather the brown Mexican cock, fucked a fifteen-year-old girl in our studio and now she's screwing us out of twenty million dollars. He has all the fun and we have to pay the fucking money. How does that grab you?"

Renata blushes hard and almost immediately becomes very pale. A hush falls over the room. No one speaks or even stirs.

"So," Watson continues without a hint that he has noticed our discomfort, "go back to whatever you do, I'm sure it's extremely important work. You might save the world. Just watch every step you take around here. Be very careful."

He gulps down the last of his coffee, snaps his briefcase closed, adjusts his drab tie, and leaves the conference room without another look.

I stagger back to the studio to continue with my shift: "I'm back, music fans." My voice is shaking badly. "In thirty minutes we'll start a new puzzle for the 'Crime in the Afternoon' contest."

5

I start to shake again while driving home. The rain is pouring. The traffic lights coming toward me down Wisconsin
Avenue are blinding. I turn onto Columbia Road. The streets
in Adams Morgan are noisier than usual, or so they seem. My
wipers aren't working well and the Metro buses are spraying
mud and gunk onto my windows. I can't look out clearly to
see where I'm driving. Maybe I have tears in my eyes. When I
get to the stop sign at Nineteenth Street, I pull down the visor
and look at myself in the little lighted mirror. My God, I look
awful! My mascara has run down my cheeks in black streaks.
Moisture has plastered my hair on my forehead, and my lipstick is half gone. No woman should ever look like this. I turn
on the radio.

Manny has been allowed to continue at the station "on
probation." Truth is, management doesn't want to lose any lis-

teners during Manny's shift. That's the only reason he's still there. However, he's not the same Manny. His voice sounds distant, lifeless, without its usual vibrancy. "The phones aren't working tonight," he announces. "Please don't call the studio. I'll play some love songs for your musical enjoyment. Hopefully the phone lines will be mended by tomorrow and we'll continue with our dedications then. Right now, let's listen to Frank Sinatra's 'One For My Baby And One More For The Road'." My heart is breaking for Manny.

I'm home. I park my little Escort in my assigned space, in back of my gray brick building. The walk down the path around the building is wet and muddy. The climb to my third floor apartment is slow and tiring today. I'm totally soaked when I walk in. The apartment looks so drab this evening. The Ben Shahn silkscreen, the one of a man standing alone and staring out at an infinite sea of blue, depresses me. I might just put it on another wall, in the small hallway to the bedroom where it won't be so prominent. I take off my shoes, my jeans and my blue denim shirt and walk around barefoot in my underwear to the bathroom.

I put my soaking clothes in the washing machine, undo my bra, take off my panties and walk into the shower. The steaming water feels so good. I think I'm going to stay under the water for a long, long time. I shampoo my hair twice and lift my face to the showerhead, letting the water scald my skin. Finally I come out. With a towel I clean the fog off the full length mirror and take a good look at myself. A hard, critical look. My mother always told me I was too vain for my own good. That I cared too much about the way I look. Maybe it is vanity although I like to think of it as a healthy competitive spirit. Mom wouldn't understand that. With her regal air, her flawless pale complexion, even at her age, with her graceful walk and perfect teeth, she doesn't understand about measuring up to others. I'm not bad. I'm not great-looking, but I'm not bad. A little on the thin side, not tall enough, not round enough. My face is a little too long. But my lips are full and pretty good-looking. My nose is short and my eyes are hazel. Not green. Not brown. They're the color of dark green olives. But I have long lashes which I emphasize with black mascara.

My breasts are not big enough and my hips are rather narrow. My mother once told me, as she was walking a few paces behind me, that I needed to put on a little weight because from behind I looked like a little boy. But when I put on a black halter top, with black tight lycra pants, and comb my hair to one side and color my lips a rich dark burgundy, I feel totally devastating. Unfortunately, I have dressed like that only once, when I went to Elaine's in New York during a National Radio convention. I was the queen of the ball after just a few martinis.

Finished with my self analysis and not feeling any better, I wrap myself in a thick white terry robe, dry my hair with a towel, and walk into the kitchen. There I pour myself a gin. I don't much like gin but I can't find anything else in the cupboard. I've had it here since I moved in. Sue gave it to me as a housewarming present. She likes gin and she likes vodka. Both taste the same to me.

It's seven-thirty, I sit on the love seat with glass in hand

and open my Criminal Law book. I have to begin studying for Monday's class so I can enjoy a free weekend. I close the book. Nothing makes sense to me. I don't understand what I'm reading. I can't study. I need to hear Manny's voice, know that he's all right. I walk over to the phone and notice that my answering machine is blinking. I push the button and listen.

"Gloria," an affable voice says, "this is Peter." My heart skips a beat. He called fifteen minutes ago when I was in the shower. "I'd like to talk to you. I have a few suggestions for your friend. I'm sorry I missed you. I'll try you in a couple of hours." Click. *Oh my God. I missed his call. What if he doesn't call again? Today is Friday.* I won't be able to see him all weekend.

I try Manny at the studio. The phone rings for a long time, with no answer. The radio is playing "Melancholy Baby." It reflects my mood. I decide to call him on the studio's business line; maybe he'll answer that line. It works: "Hello, WVVV-FM" he barks into the phone.

"It's me, Manny, Gloria. Are you O.K.? Did you read my note? My law professor is looking into your problem."

"I can't talk to you, Gloria. I'm so goddamn mad about what that bastard Halifax did to me today. Sending that goddamn attorney. He embarrassed me in front of the whole goddamn station. Everybody's talking about it. Even some of my listeners heard about it from gossip at the station and have been calling me. I'm dying here. I hate that bastard. I'm so goddamn mad, I don't know what to do. I'll talk to you tomorrow." Click.

"Manny, Manny." It's no use. I go to the kitchen and bite

into some cold chicken. It doesn't taste right. And the bread is three days old. I make myself a sandwich anyway.

At ten-thirty p.m. the phone rings.

"Peter?" I ask.

"Who's Peter?" It's my mother, calling from Florida. "Why haven't I heard about him before? And why would he be calling so late?"

"He'd be calling late because he had a meeting."

"Still waiting for your Prince Charming, darling? I already told you many times he doesn't exist. You know, it's getting time for you to think about settling down. . ."

"Yes, Ma. How are you and Daddy? I miss you both." I love my mother, but I want to hurry her off the phone; if Peter phones on call waiting I'll have to explain to her why I'm hanging up on her.

"Then why don't you come visit? It's wonderful here. How about coming for Thanksgiving?"

"I can't. I already told my program director I would take over the shifts of other people who are married, so they can spend the holiday with their families."

"Gloria, you don't look after yourself."

"Yes I do, Ma. I really do. Please don't worry."

"You know I always worry about you. Are you eating all right, sweetie? Are you exercising?"

"Yes, Ma."

"What's wrong, baby?"

"There's nothing wrong, Ma! I'm just tired. I've been working very hard. I'm going to sleep very soon."

"Okay, darling. Please call us tomorrow. Your Daddy's asleep already. He wants to hear your voice."

"I will, Ma."

"I love you, baby. Get some rest. I hope Peter calls you. He's a fool if he doesn't."

I've got to smile. "I love you, too. Good night, Ma."

My mother. Such a nice woman. But tough. Tough and rational. With her, right is right and wrong is wrong. No two ways about it. I'm more open, less judgmental. I let my instincts carry me on occasion. She loves my father. He adores her. I think I'm seeking what my mother and father have. I want a man who smiles every time he sees me come into the room, the way my father smiles–almost imperceptibly–when he sees my cute mother. I want a man whose life revolves around mine.

I'm half lying on the couch, law book in hand. The only thing I'm wearing is my half-open bathrobe. It has stopped raining. My one glass of gin has turned into two or three glasses. The chicken is still on my plate. It looks so unappetizing.

The phone startles me. I lean to pick it up and my bathrobe opens up.

"Gloria, it's Peter. Is it too late to call? I went out to dine with some friends and we just finished."

"No, Peter, of course it's not too late." *Friends, he said. Not wife. Not we.* "I was just studying."

"Studying. At ten-forty five on a Friday night? A pretty girl like you? I don't believe it."

"Peter, would you like to come over and. . . and. . . talk to me about. . . about my friend?" I sound like an idiot. Like a

50

total idiot. My voice, my best feature, sounds like the voice of a teenager–high, shrill, unsophisticated.

"Now?" he asks.

"Now."

"Where do you live?"

I can't believe it. He might actually come and see me. But I'm a mess and the apartment matches.

"2093 Kalorama Road. Do you know where that is?"

"In Adams Morgan? I'm just a few minutes away. We ate at Kinkead's on Pennsylvania Avenue. I'll be there in fifteen minutes."

"It can be hard to park around here."

"Don't worry, my friends are driving me. They'll drop me off. See you soon."

I jump off the couch. Put the plate with the cold chicken in the kitchen. I have nothing to offer him to drink. Just a small amount of gin left over. I brush my teeth and comb my hair as well I can, put on a short silk robe. I take it off. Put on a long-sleeved jumpsuit. I take it off. I finally end up with a white T shirt, a pair of tight black jeans–I like the way they emphasize my butt–and a pair of high-heeled white sandals. I want to look sexy and taller and more beautiful. My heart is racing. I have no underwear on.

The bell rings.

"I'd like to have a word or two with your friend, kiddo, the one who's in trouble about the rape. When can we see him?" Peter is walking and taking in the whole apartment. "Hey, this is nice, very nice. I like your art." He throws his jacket on a chair in the small dining room facing the balcony.

"My parents gave me almost everything you see here." I'd like to tell him to go look at the signed Picasso lithograph hanging over my bed. It really is the nicest piece of art I own. But it would sound so obvious, so provocative. I bite my tongue. We talk for a while about my parents and their life in Florida. I still don't know anything about his life. I'm afraid to ask too much.

"I've been listening to your show, Gloria," he says while making himself comfortable on the love seat.

I sit close to him. "Thank you. Do you like it?"

"You sound good. Quite a sexy voice." He doesn't move away.

I can't stop smiling. "Tell me more."

"Well, that crime contest you have going. . . pretty simple stuff, wouldn't you say?"

I'm a little stung but I hide it. Instead, I pour the last drops from the bottle of gin and offer him my glass. I sit back and move just a little closer to him. "I have to make it simple at the beginning to make it easy for my listeners. The easier it is, the more people want to play. It'll become harder and harder until the end when I have to create a real tough one. Could you help me come up with a real crime for my listeners to solve? You worked at the D.A.'s office, didn't you?"

"Yes."

"You must have a million interesting cases you can share with me."

"Sure, sure. When the time comes. Tell me about your Detective Sabrina. That was an interesting voice."

"You mean–Good afternoon, Gloria, I'll tell you about today's crime." I imitate Irma's low purring voice. I'm good at imitating voices. Very, very good. It's one of my few talents. I look at Peter and smile. He smiles back.

"Hey," he says. "It was you all the time. There is no Detective Sabrina." He sounds disappointed.

"No, no, she's Irma Halifax, the owner's wife. Just as beautiful and exotic as she sounds." I lean closer to Peter. He doesn't pull away.

"You smell of soap and shampoo," he says. "I like it."

I wish I were still wearing my robe and I could let it open -just a bit. Let him look at my thighs, take a peek at my breasts. The thought of it makes me giggle. I inhale his aroma of cologne mixed with cigar. I like the way he smells. I'm getting very drunk with the gin and with Peter's smell and his presence and his navy blue cashmere sweater rubbing against my shoulder and my cheek. My eyes are half closed. I know we should be discussing Manny, but I just can't concentrate. My feelings for Peter are so warm, so intoxicating. My skin is tingling.

"Peter," I whisper, "Peter, I need. . . "

"Babe, I know what you need." He lifts me slowly from the couch and he holds me carefully by me underarms. I lean against him and rub my breast against his arm. We start walking the small corridor toward my bedroom.

"Is this the right way?"

I nod. He walks me to my bedroom. Gently, very gently he lays me down on the bed. He pulls my shirt off, takes off my sandals and slips my jeans off. I close my eyes. I feel him bending down close to me, his breath coming closer to my face. He kisses my forehead. Then I feel him slowly pulling the covers over my naked body.

I open my eyes to the sound of the front door gently closing behind him.

6

"Ladies and gentlemen, I'm sorry to interrupt our regularly scheduled program to bring you this breaking news. Here now is WVVV news director, Tim Elias. Good afternoon, Tim."

"Good afternoon, Gloria. We've just learned that the President collapsed and was rushed to Walter Reed Hospital. We'll take you now to the White House for a message from the Vice President, followed by a press conference." Tim switches us to the Vice President. I'm in the studio waiting for half an hour to continue with my show. I'm sure that by now all of my audience has dwindled to nothing.

"This is Tim Elias, WVVV news. And now here is Gloria."

"Thank you, Tim. It's good to hear that the President will make a full recovery. We're half an hour late for our contest, but we still have fifteen minutes to play. I don't want to deprive anyone of the chance to win today's thousand-dollar prize. Detective Sabrina is waiting patiently for our call. So let's call her and listen to the clue of the day. Good luck and good hunting." I dial Irma's number and let it ring two or three times. I put on a commercial and run out to her office to prompt her to pick up the phone. She's not there, however. The script I left on her desk is still there. I grab it and run back to the studio, turn on the mike and in my best imitation ever, I coo:

"Good afternoon, Gloria, this is Detective Sabrina."

I answer myself: "Good afternoon, Detective, welcome to our show. Please tell us about today's Crime in the Afternoon."

Back to Irma's voice: "Yes, with pleasure. The puzzle goes like this. Mr. Smith, a partner in the bakery of Smith and Lowe, claims he was robbed while he was alone in the store. He claims that the thief took all the money in the safe and in the register. Mr. Smith said he saw the thief's face only for a moment before he was blindfolded. He took the blindfold off only after he heard the thief slam the front door shut. After Mr. Smith pointed out the thief, he himself was apprehended. Do you think that's enough of a hint, Gloria?"

I answer: "It's enough for tonight, Detective Sabrina. Let's keep 'em guessing. Maybe we'll have a true Perry Mason calling with the correct answer before my shift is over. Folks, you now have fourteen minutes to come up with the correct answer. I have a thousand dollars in my pocket waiting for you."

I finish my little charade with no callers. It's not a good evening. My plans are shot for the evening. I'm feeling very despondent. Manny asked me to take his shift tonight; he said he had an emergency to attend to. Didn't specify. I'm upset that I'll miss my Monday night law class and I won't see Peter. I haven't heard from him since he tucked me into bed Friday night. But I couldn't say no to Manny's request, under the circumstances.

"Ladies and gents, I'll have another clue for you tomorrow afternoon. I hope we'll have a winner. It's six o'clock and I'm happy to report to you that after the news I'll be back to play some love songs that Manny the Silver Fox left for you."

Sue comes running into the studio, breathless, while the news is on.

I whistle when I see her: "Boy oh boy, Sue, you look incredibly elegant in that pant suit. It really looks good on you. Turquoise looks fabulous on you. Hot date tonight, eh?"

"I wish," she sighs. "I'm supposed to be at the opening of the glass retrospective of Martin Sergei at Walter's gallery. Walter's sponsoring him. He begged me to be there tonight, to help him greet the guests. Robert Verona, Mr. Halifax's chauffeur, was supposed to pick me up at five-thirty. I've been waiting in the street for half an hour and the guy never showed up. I need to grab a taxi but I don't have enough money with me. Can you please lend me five or ten bucks?"

"Certainly. What time is the opening?"

"It's starts at six. With the traffic the way it is now it's going to take me at least forty-five minutes to get there.

Walter's going to kill me. He wanted me to be there with him to welcome the crowd."

I hand her a twenty-dollar bill. "Will this be enough?"

"Thanks, I'm sure it is. I'll pay you back tomorrow. By the way, how come you're still here? I thought you had a law class tonight."

"Manny asked me to fill in for him for a little while," I lie. "He had some emergency to take care of. He'll be back soon."

"Well, I don't especially love it that you're here alone, but Mr. Jenkins is already at his post. I just saw him. He was listening to your show. Bye, sweetie, wish me luck. I need a taxi. And don't forget to lock the front door after me. There's nobody left in the place."

Out she runs.

I'm miffed that I wasn't invited to Walter's opening. Having class on Mondays, I'm not sure I would have gone, but I'm miffed anyway. I went to Walter's gallery last Saturday morning to look at the art pieces that were being placed. Saturdays are usually lonely days for me. When I woke up last Saturday I decided it was time to be brave and give Peter a call. Just to hear his voice. What I really wanted was to find out, once and for all, whether he's married. And if he isn't, boy oh boy, I'm going to make a play for him. I'm going to make him really fall for me. The only thing I need is a plan, of course. So I called information and to my great delight I found out that he lives in D.C., just a few minutes from my apartment. I thanked the operator effusively and stared at his phone number for a while. Kissed the piece of paper and put it in my pocket. It was definitely too early to call. Maybe later, I thought. Maybe tomorrow. I still haven't called him.

Since I was feeling lonely and forlorn after my failed attempt at seducing Peter, I did what I always do when I'm feeling low, visit art galleries, especially glass art galleries. I love glass art. It's so whimsical, so personal. It changes colors with the changing light and it looks so fragile, so intriguing and so powerful at the same time. My parents have been collecting glass art for many years and have some wonderful pieces. I have a few of my own, not expensive ones, just a few of local artists, mostly students at the Corcoran Gallery. So I went to Walter's gallery, "The Glass Peacock." Just to look. It's a very impressive gallery. Perfect to show the best contemporary glass artists. The one-room gallery is spacious, very bright, very classy and expensive. It fills me with a sense of awe and wonder the moment I walk into it.

Walter is Mr. Halifax's younger son. He has tried his hand at various businesses. Sue has told me, with a great deal of relish, of his failed attempt to run one of Mr. Halifax's stations, the one on the eastern shore of Maryland. Apparently he spent most of his time at the bars on the beach. The staff there was up in arms. So his father brought him back to D.C. and hired a new manager there to do the job.

Walter is a handsome devil. He's probably in his early thirties. He has a gap-toothed smile that glistens, a dimpled chin, dark hair cut very stylishly, very glossy, very sexy. His green eyes sparkle when he laughs; they make him look impish, child-like. Every time I see him, and it's not been too often–even though he has a small office at the station–he looks spiffy. He wears tailored clothes, cashmere turtleneck, and Italian loafers. The first time I saw him–it must be two years ago, only a few weeks after I started working here–he was walking through the halls of the station, slapping people on the back, laughing his boyish laugh. I couldn't believe my eyes. What a hunk. I looked him up and down and when I got down to his loafers I saw he wasn't wearing socks. It had never happened to me before; the jolt of seeing his naked ankles, his naked insteps, had the same physical effect on me as if he had caressed my breasts. With his lips. I had a hard time falling asleep that night.

Sue told me that Walter has a problem holding onto a job. Any job. She told me he graduated from a fancy private high school near the bottom of his class and that his career at the University of Maryland lasted only two years of partying hard at his fraternity. His father had to bail him out of a narcotics charge and he was asked to leave the university. Nothing seemed to interest Walter except partying, drinking, and drugs.

When he hit upon the idea of opening a glass art gallery, Mr. Halifax backed him financially with a loan. Sue told me it wasn't simply a loan. There are several strings attached to it. He has to live at home, so that his father can keep an eye on him; he has to succeed at the gallery and treat it as a real business; and he has to lay off drugs. If he doesn't adhere to all of that, all the money will be taken away from him. All of it. His entire inheritance will go to his older brother Patrick, a stockbroker in New York. Patrick graduated from Princeton and got his MBA from Wharton. He just married his college sweetheart, Samantha, also a stockbroker. Together they opened a stock brokerage firm that is becoming the rage in New York.

The "Glass Peacock," Walter's gallery, is his pride and joy. He holds openings every two months for established artists like Danny Perkins or Richard Royal. Occasionally he hosts receptions for new, promising artists. The openings are elegant, elaborate affairs. I was invited to the one prior to this one. I guess Walter overheard me talking about glass artists and was surprised at how much I like their art. The opening was lavish–champagne, caviar, a quintet playing soft jazz. Every sculpture was perfectly lit. The wooden floors had been polished to a high gloss. The walls were painted a soft pink to highlight the bright blue and purple hues of Yvette La Fontaine's whimsical cat-like sculptures. It was a kaleidoscope of colors. A video of the artist at work was prominently displayed. Walter himself, dressed in a tux, welcomed every guest. He really seemed to be enjoying the evening immensely. I don't know if anything was sold. The prices were so high it would have taken half my yearly salary of twenty-five thousand dollars to buy just one piece. It was a very entertaining evening nevertheless.

With Sue gone, the studio is very lonely. Very quiet. I miss Peter and wish I could've gone to his class. Around seven-thirty, as I'm putting on a Barbra Streisand CD, I hear the front door to the station open. It startles me. Manny's shift is from six to midnight and I'm supposed to be alone in the station until a few minutes before midnight. I've taken over his shift a couple of times. Paul Scott, the overnight deejay, usually shows up–disheveled and out of breath–just a minute or two before his shift starts.

Manny walks into the studio looking dejected. His eyes are downcast as he walks toward me. I've never seen him like this.

"Manny, what are you doing here?" I ask. "Did you take care of your emergency already? I thought I wasn't going to see you all evening."

"I'll take over for you now," he says. His voice is flat. "You can go to your class."

"It's too late, Manny. I'd never make it on time. Can I keep you company here? You don't seem to be yourself."

"Uh, oh . . . O.K. . . . I don't know . . .Maybe it would be better if I were alone."

I put on a fresh CD without even announcing it. I've gone outside of the rotation he had left for me and I forgot to air the commercials. The sales department will be complaining bitterly about me tomorrow. But I just forgot to do it.

I get up from my deejay chair, take off the earphones, walk over to Manny, take his hand and lead him to the chair. I stand behind him and clutch his head to my chest. Hard. I caress his silky black hair. I love the way it feels. He doesn't react to me at all.

"What's happening, Manny? Where were you?"

I can see his reflection on the glass wall. He looks forlorn. His opens his mouth to say something, pushes his long hair away from his eye and turns and looks at me. He just shakes his head.

"Please talk to me," I plead. "Maybe I can help."

"You wouldn't understand, Gloria. Please let me finish my shift."

"Is there anything I can do for you?" I'm pressing too hard. "Do you need anything?"

"I don't need anything right now." He says. "Thanks anyway. Please go now."

He puts on an Ella Fitzgerald CD, "The Man I Love"–with no introduction, no dedication. The phones are ringing continuously, but he lets the machine answer.

"Any news from your friend, the professor?" he asks.

"Not yet. I'm waiting to hear from him. I'll let you know as soon as he comes up with something."

"Thank's. You're a good friend." He takes my hand and slowly brings it to his lips. They're soft lips. Warm lips. I want this moment to last for a long time. My heart is pounding, my mouth is dry.

"Manny . . ."

"Please go home, Gloria. Let me finish my shift," he says very softly.

"Music fans, please call me with your requests. I'm back. The Silver Fox is at your service. And now, for Dick with undying love from Paula, this one's for you."

I walk out of the studio quietly. Mr. Jenkins is sitting on his bench, leaning against the wall. He has a small radio against his ear. He's listening to Manny and smiling.

Gisela Huberman

I call Peter as soon as I get home. I let it ring until the answering machine picks up. But I don't leave a message.

7

Sleep eludes me even though it's been a long, exhausting Monday. I toss and turn and try to think of Peter. But my mind keeps going back to Manny. I try to understand his uncharacteristic mood and behavior at the station this evening. I was listening to his show while getting ready to go to bed. It didn't sound like him. The voice was too strained. The usual quips and short little poems were missing. "From Ron with love to Eve." Period. No saucy remarks. No underlying sexual innuendo. No fun. I turned it off. Pulled the blanket over me and closed my eyes

The phone rings. *My God. It's Peter. Thank you, God.* I want to hear his voice. I want his presence.

"Hello, hello. . ."

"Hi Gloria, it's me, Sue. I didn't wake you, did I?" She starts giggling. Sue doesn't giggle. She commands. She asks.

She orders. I've never heard Sue giggle before.

"Sue, hi. No, you didn't wake me. What's up?"

"Well, I heard that Manny was back on the air, so I just wanted to know how it went for you tonight." She giggles again.

"Sue, are you all right?"

"I'm peachy." *Peachy?* "I'm coming over to your place right now. I want to tell you something."

"Now? It's almost midnight."

"So what? We can have ourselves a girls' party. Just you and me. And a couple of bottles. Do you have anything to drink? Never mind. I'll bring us a nice picnic basket. With something nice for us to drink. Don't you worry. We'll have us a nice girlie party. It's going to be fun."

"Sue, how are you getting here? Parking is impossible around here." I'm trying hard to discourage the party.

"Don't worry about it. I'll grab a cab. I owe you twenty dollars. I'll bring it over. Are you ready to party?" Giggles. She hangs up.

I'm struggling out of bed. It's been a long day. Whatever interesting news Sue has to share apparently can't wait until tomorrow. Well then, let's make it a fun party. I put on a robe and smooth my hair. I cut a few pieces of cheddar cheese, open a jar of green olives, and put some salmon spread on wheat crackers. I didn't eat anything for dinner and suddenly feel very hungry. I nibble on some cheese while waiting for Sue. What I'm really doing is waiting for Peter to call! Or at least hoping he will.

"How was it, Sue?" I ask as soon as she steps into my apartment "How was the opening?" She's flushed, her dark shoulder-length hair, usually stiff, is tousled. Her jeans are very tight and her white cotton blouse is open a few buttons, revealing a glimpse of her breasts. *Wow*, I think. It's quite interesting to me how beautiful women don't realize how really beautiful they look simply dressed. Sue is a knockout dressed like this.

"Oh, Gloria," she gushes, setting a large shopping bag on the dining table. "The opening was great, just great. The glass pieces were incredible. The food was wonderful. Everything was perfect. Just perfect." She's beaming. I'm jealous.

"Were there lots of people?" I want to know everything about the evening.

"It was packed," she says, taking a bottle out of the bag. "Here let's have a drink or two." She skips over to the cupboard in my tiny kitchen and takes out two glasses, puts ice into them from my freezer, and pours vodka over the ice. "Here, drink."

"Tell me about Walter. Did he look fabulous? Who was he with"?

"Well, I didn't see him there. I don't think he was there."

"What? I don't believe it. I heard he never misses one of his openings."

"Well, I didn't see him. I got there a little after six thirty and he wasn't there. I only stayed about forty five minutes. Maybe he arrived after I left. Who knows? I found a very nice ride to take me home, though. Ron Douglas, a Congressman's legislative aide who was kind enough to give me a lift." She winks and giggles.

It's embarrassing seeing her so out of character. "What happened?" I ask.

"Just a little kiss, a sweet little hug, nothing more than that. But we're going to the Kennedy Center to hear the National Symphony on Saturday. After that, who knows?"

"That's great Sue. I'm very happy for you." *I am very happy for her.* "I wonder what happened to Walter. Could he have been sick?"

"Who knows? The gallery was a madhouse and people were still pouring in when Ron and I left. I must have missed him in the crowd."

"Too bad. I wanted to hear all the sexy details about Walter."

"You really like Walter, huh?"

"He's so handsome, so easygoing, so charming."

"So out of your league, my friend." *That hurts, but I won't let her see it.* "But now, let me tell you a little about Ron." She's sitting on the couch, her legs propped comfortably on my glass coffee table. "I think I could really like the man. Really like him. Uhmmm." She takes a very long swig of the vodka "Yummm." She takes a piece of cheese and a pitted olive. Pops one after the other into her mouth. "You really are a very good cook, you know that, Gloria? I've told you that before, haven't I?"

Sue and I have been friends for a long time. Well, I wouldn't exactly call us friends. She's been my boss, she's been good to me; she's been my mentor. And I've been a good employee. Have caused her no problems. Always ready and always on time. We've had dinners together and sometimes we've gone to a bar together for a nightcap. But we've never traded any intimate secrets the way real friends do. I respect her, I admire her. But she doesn't know anything about my private life. And neither do I about hers.

I've worked for Sue since I was in college, at American University, in the Communications department. She was the manager of the university's radio station. Then she left to become the general manager of a small station owned by Halifax in New Bern, North Carolina, and when I graduated I followed her there. We both escaped New Bern as soon as possible. Mr. Halifax, was so happy with Sue's performance at the station, that he transferred her to WVVV in D.C., her old haunts, and she took me with her. With all the connections she had made while at American University, she made WVVV flourish in the ratings and because of that it has became a great financial success.

In all the years we've known each other, I've never seen Sue so loose, so talkative, so drunk, in such tight jeans. In fact, I've never seen her dressed in anything other than her business suits with long jackets that cover her hips–such slim hips, why cover them?–and that fit loosely, so that I never even knew she had such a good-looking pair of breasts. Every time she moves tonight, the blouse opens a bit and I peek at them. I can see them quite clearly in her open, unbuttoned shirt. Good-looking breasts. Hard looking. Soft looking too. Nice round nipples. *Hey, what am I doing? She's a woman! Well, I'm just comparing. She wins.*

"Hey kid," she says, and as she turns toward me, the

blouse opens a bit–there we go again with the peek-a-boo breasts. "You know, I've never really been in love? Really in love? Crazy in love? Ron may be it. Cute, cute guy. Very manly, you know? Good kisser. I'm not a prude. Never have been. Never will be. But jumping in bed with just anyone is not my style. Ron, however, really made my juices flow, you know what I mean?"

"Yes, Sue," I say, "I know what you mean."

"I would've pushed him into bed tonight. I would've jumped on his bones. I wanted him to touch me, to make me feel wanted, attractive. I wanted him so much. Maybe it was the champagne or his cologne. But no, I don't think so. He was just so yummy. And the more I wanted to. . ." She closes her eyes, holds the glass of vodka and ice close to her cheek and turns silent.

There's a long silence between us.

"Sue, have you ever gone to bed with Mr. Halifax?" I blurt out. It's been on my mind for a long time; their easy camaraderie, everything she knows about him and his family. I don't think you could know so much about your boss unless you were on intimate terms.

She stares at me for a long time. Her eyes are bloodshot and her lips are closed very tightly. I don't know if she's mad at me for asking her something she has never revealed before or if she's thinking about divulging a secret. She finally lets out a small laugh.

"Kid, you're too smart for your own good." Is that a confession? "You remember when he came to New Bern and we had late meetings?"

"Yes, I remember." I smile.

"We were making love in his hotel room all night long. A man his age. It was always oral sex, though. He didn't want to make a mistake, as he called it. I never once felt him inside me. Not once. I didn't mind, though. As a matter of fact, now that I think about it, I'm sure I liked it. Especially the attention he gave me before and after. But there was no passion to it. At least not from my side. Then, all of a sudden, a couple of years ago, maybe four years ago it stopped. Just like that." She snapped her fingers. "I haven't been with him since then. He dropped me just like that, without an explanation. Without a reason. Well, maybe he had a reason. He met someone else. The bastard. And I introduced her to him. Goddamn bastard. And he dropped me. Just like that. A true gentleman. The bastard. I was not real pleased about it. I even thought about quitting working for him. But then," she sighs "what would I gain? He's always called all the shots." Sue hands me her empty glass. Her eyes are misty, her hands shaking slightly. "Here, fill it up again to the top."

"You really think you ought to have more?"

"Just fill it to the top! I'm telling things I never dared tell anyone. I need something to keep me going. It's been quite lonely, you know."

I get up, go to the kitchen, put some fresh ice in the glass and fill it again with vodka. I've never seen Sue drink like this. I get back to her. She's standing in front of the entrance mirror looking at herself intently. "What do you think? Horrible looking?" She turns her face to the right and then to the left; she smooths her hair and opens her white blouse a bit more.

"Sue, you know you're a very good-looking woman. And smart. And accomplished. I think you're what every woman dreams of becoming." I mean every word of it.

"You really are a good kid. No wonder I like you so much. Tell me, what do you know about Halifax?"

"He's rich, he's old, he's married to Irma. I work for him and he has a bunch of radio stations and cable and newspapers. That's about all I know."

"You want to know more?" Sue sips her vodka and doesn't wait for an answer. She sits back on the couch, holds the glass with both hands, between her legs, turns slightly toward me, and with an impish smile says: "Hold on to your seat, it's going to be a bumpy ride." Not a bad imitation of Bette Davis.

"His father committed suicide."

"Oh, my God. Why?"

"He was found in the bathroom of the House of Lords in a compromising situation with a young man. He was a famous and controversial man, John Halifax, Duke of Buckingham or something, member of the House of Lords for many years. He was very conservative in his views and made a fair number of enemies. He apparently also suffered from a disease. Tourette's syndrome. I'm sure you've heard of it."

I nod.

"Well, our Mr. Halifax told me that the disease makes you start shouting obscenities, among other things. So, it seems that old John Halifax suffered an attack witnessed by some reporters and some of his political enemies. His faults were duly reported in the tabloid papers, together with that small incident in the bathroom with the young man. So it seems his pride couldn't take all that publicity, I guess, and he killed himself. Exit."

"How old was our Mr. H. when all this happened?"

"Old Vince. Well, I'm not really sure. I think he was about nineteen or twenty. He was at Oxford. He was the oldest of three boys. Their mother was so devastated by the suicide and all the publicity around the whole affair that she left London, retired to their country home and lost interest in life."

"And what did our Mr. H. do?"

"He decided to come to the good ol' U.S.A., so people wouldn't know about his genetics and about the family disgrace and all the shame the family was going through. He decided to come here to make a fresh start, so to speak."

"Does Mr. H. have the same disease his father had?"

"I don't know. But his kids could surely inherit it. Any one of his kids."

"Oh boy. Does Walter know about this?"

"I suppose so. If I know about it, I don't see why Walter wouldn't. So, to finish the story, Vincent came to this country with a small inheritance his father left him, quickly became a citizen, bought a small radio station when he was in his late twenties, sold it for a nice profit, bought more and the rest is history."

"He has done well for himself."

"I'll say!"

Sue drains the last drops of vodka, stretches her arms over her head and says: "Boy, I'm bushed. What time is it?"

"It's three a.m."

"Jesus Christ. We've a programming staff meeting tomorrow at nine a.m. sharp. With the entire programming staff. God! And I'm not ready. Look at me. What a mess. I'd better be going, kiddo."

I nod. "There's an all-night taxi stand at the corner."

She gets up with a little jump. She really should be wearing jeans more often–she looks quite sexy. She walks over to me, caresses my cheek lightly, adjusts her blouse and slowly walks to the door. From behind, she looks twenty-five. She must be in her early forties. I wonder how she does it.

The screech of the phone shatters my sensuous dream. I can barely open my eyes to look at the clock on the night stand. It's six in the morning. God, only three hours of sleep! I'm so groggy I can't even find the phone.

"Hello." I'm hoarse from lack of sleep and too much alcohol.

"Gloria–He's dead." Sue's sobbing hysterically.

"Sue, Sue, I can't understand you. What are you saying? Are you dreaming? What are you talking about?"

"Gloria," she screams in my ear, "Halifax is dead. He's been killed. Murdered. Watson, his attorney, just called me. My God, oh God. What are we going to do? Come pick me up. I can't drive." She hangs up with a loud thud.

Shakily I spring out of bed. Can't think straight. I'm totally bewildered and can't focus on what to do. I throw some clothes on and sprint down the three floors to the street. God, it's freezing outside. I've no idea where my car is. There it is, behind the building, where I always park it. I zoom down Connecticut Avenue to Georgetown, where Sue's small townhouse is. I've been there many times for meetings and cocktail parties, but don't recognize the streets today. They don't seem to be the same. After getting lost a couple of times, I'm finally in Sue's neighborhood. As I approach her house, I can see a slumped body on the front steps. My heart is paralyzed from fear and my body is totally drenched. I can feel my undershirt and pants sticking to my skin. Is it Sue? Is she all right? I jump out of the car and run toward her house. Her head is buried in her arms. She's clutching her knees and her body is convulsing spasmodically. She doesn't even know I'm there. I sit beside her and hug her hard.

"Oh my God, Gloria, why, why?" she sobs.

8

We have to maintain a semblance of normalcy for our radio listeners. We can't allow the panic inside our walls to go out over the air.

The morning team of the famous Jay and Mark Show are doing their usual Tuesday morning routine of "A day in the life of . . ." calling out to the audience. They are waiting to hear from caller number ten to give away tickets to the Redskins game. These are coveted tickets even when the 'Skins are having a very bad year. Mr. Halifax had long-standing Redskins season tickets that he allowed the station to give away once in a while. The contest was wildly popular. And it is going very well today. No one can tell from listening to the two seasoned deejays that there is anything wrong at the station. They are pros.

The Jay and Mark Show finished at nine in the morning,

in time for our scheduled programming staff meeting. The meeting never came to pass.

Beyond the studio's sounds, however, the whole station is in disarray. The phones are ringing constantly, police detectives are milling about, and the press is asking for interviews. The press is particularly interested in finding out the future of Halifax's radio empire. Sue has locked herself in her office; I hear her sobbing every time I walk past her office. I'm just pacing up and down the hallways. There's chaos everywhere I turn.

Arnold Watson, Halifax's attorney, marches into the station mid-morning. An unlit cigarette is hanging from his lips. He calls for a quick staff meeting of those "who are milling around in the station doing nothing." He stands at the head of the mahogany table, matchbooks, cigarette boxes, pens, and pencils spilling out of every pocket of his open briefcase. He carefully places the unlit cigarette in the breast pocket of his rumpled suit, takes a swig of coffee, and says in his booming voice:

"Now, it's up to every single one of you to keep this place operating in perfect order. We must keep Mr. Halifax's investments intact. For Irma's sake and for Mr. Halifax's two sons. You have a great general manager here. I'm sure she'll be able to lead you capably, as she has always done."

He gestures grandly in Sue's direction. She's pale and drawn with two huge black circles under her eyes. She has managed to comb her hair reasonably well and has dabbed some lipstick on, but her anxiety shows in her forlorn gaze. She manages a weak smile when she realizes that Watson is talking about her and sits up a little straighter. But her eyes are pools of anguish.

"First thing, ladies and gentlemen," Watson continues, "is focus, focus. Focus on your duties. None of you here are going to lose your jobs if you just follow a few simple rules. We're a good radio station and we're going to continue to be good. The police are hot on the trail of the murderous bastard. I'm sure they'll want to talk to you and I expect each one of you to cooperate fully. You'd better. For your own sake. And one more thing, nothing of what takes place here should leave these walls. Whoever blabs gets skewered. I hope I'm making myself perfectly clear. Not one word outside these walls."

He snaps his briefcase closed, takes a quick gulp of coffee, slams the coffee cup on the mahogany table, and stalks out of the conference room without another word or glance.

It's two o'clock. I have to go on the air. I feel dizzy. I put on the CDs, announce the name of the singer, run commercials and listen to Tim Elias read the news. Every movement I make and every word I say seems surreal. I can see and hear myself doing things, uttering words, but I don't know whether they make any sense or not.

At five-fifteen I start the "Crime in the Afternoon" contest. It sounds ghoulish to me. But we're supposed to do our jobs as if everything were normal.

"Loyal music fans, we're about to start our contest." *Is this my own voice? I don't recognize it at all.* "After the following commercial announcement, I'll provide the second clue. Nobody solved it yesterday. The prize is now seven-hundred and fifty dollars for the first correct answer. Because of unforseen circumstances Detective Sabrina will not be with us this afternoon. She's been called by Scotland Yard to help them solve some crimes over in London. We'll certainly miss her here." I don't know how else to explain Irma's absence, and I just can't force myself to imitate her purring, sexy, low-pitched voice at this moment.

The commercial I put on is for dog food. Puppies are yelping in the background. The phone in the studio rings.

"I know you're alone. I follow your movements. This is your secret admirer again." *Oh, no. Not again. Not today. I really don't need this now.* "Thank you for calling, sir." Always polite. Might be he's a listener who's keeping a ratings book. I can't afford to lose even this listener. It could mean the difference between being number one in the ratings or being left behind with the rest of the pack. "I really can't talk to you now. The contest is about to start." *Think, think. Whose voice is that? Whose voice is that?*

"Screw the contest. Talk to me. Whisper to me. I love your voice. I want to feel you're talking only to me. That you belong to me. You're a very pretty girl, you know that?"

"Thank you, sir. I've got to get back to my show."

"Don't you dare hang up on me!" His voice frightens me. I'm trying to recognize it but I can't. It's menacing and angry.

"Things aren't right at the station, are they, little miss know-it-all?"

I hang up the phone. My voice is shaking. "Dear afternoon sleuths, this is the second clue in the case of the unknown thief. Mr. Smith, the baker, claims the robber was the famous Bobby Blue, whom nobody has ever seen. All that's known about him is that he wears a satin jacket with a gold letter B embroidered on the back. The police promptly arrested Mr. Smith. Why? Please call me as soon as you figure this one out. I have seven-hundred and fifty bucks burning my pocket. I want to give them to you."

I can't wait to finish my shift. I want this day to be over. Forty-three minutes to go. . . Forty-two. The phone in the studio rings. "Do you have an answer to the puzzle?" I ask, trying to sound as cheerful as possible, even though the call isn't broadcast unless I switch to "speaker."

"The only answer I have is to tell you to be very very careful on your way home tonight, my little missy." He hangs up.

Maybe it's time for me to tell Sue about these calls. The phone rings again. I hesitate and then answer it, "Yes?"

"Gloria, I have the answer," the caller says. I immediately switch to "speaker." "The police arrested Mr. Smith because he stole the partnership's money."

"That's absolutely correct. And how do we know it?"

"Because he said he was blindfolded before the thief turned his back. He never saw the thief's back so he couldn't have seen the embroidered B on the jacket."

"Congratulations! We have a winner, folks," I announce. "A seven-hundred-and-fifty-dollars winner whose name will be entered in the grand contest for the WVVV Jaguar convertible. Please stay on the line, caller. Veronica will take your name and address. Again, congratulations!"

The tape with the six o'clock news is on. My shift is over.

Finally. Almost everyone in the station has left. I walk over to Sue's office. Maybe we can have dinner together. Her office is locked. On my way out I peek into Manny's office. He's sitting quietly at his desk. He doesn't look up. He's preparing for his show and I don't want to disturb him. He's pale and uncharacteristically unkempt. I notice his hand is trembling as he jots down notes for his show. I put on my jacket, tie my blue wool scarf around my neck, and start walking slowly toward the door. I feel apprehensive. That creep's call left me feeling very uneasy. I walk warily to the elevator bank to go down to the basement garage. I punch the down button and wait. The door opens, revealing a man of about twenty-five, all bundled up and just standing there looking at me. He's not coming out. The station occupies the top floor of the building. Why is anybody in the elevator if he's not coming into the station? He stares at me and I hesitate. "Going down, miss?" he asks quite impatiently. I don't recognize the voice. But still I'm not able to move. "No, no, I forgot something. Sorry."

As soon as the elevator doors close, I run to Mr. Jenkins, who's listening to the news on his little portable radio. He looks up at me. "Trouble, Miss Gloria?"

"No, no, Mr. Jenkins. It's just that. . . with everything that happened. . . Would you mind terribly walking me to my car? After a day like today, even the shadows scare me."

"I'm not supposed to leave my seat here in front of the door, but I don't think a five-minute absence will create a great tragedy. Come, let's go, Miss Gloria."

"Thanks."

"I'm real sorry about what happened to Mr. Halifax. Never had the opportunity to meet him. Heard he was a great gentleman."

"He was, Mr. Jenkins. He was. It's a great loss to all of us."

We walk together and wait by the elevator. "I really like your contest," he says. "I listen to your program the minute I get here at five." We ride down to the garage, chatting amiably the whole ride. I don't want to appear frightened.

"Thank you so much, Mr. Jenkins. I appreciate a good word from my audience."

"Even from an old man like me?"

"Especially from an intelligent gentleman like you," I smile and look around. The garage always looks so empty at this hour.

"I like especially the way you do voices, of the thieves and the victims," he says. "It's very theatrical."

"Thanks, again. You're so kind. This is my car. I really appreciate your walking with me."

"Is there a problem, Miss Gloria? You don't sound right. Anything else I can do to help?"

"No, no, Mr. Jenkins. Everything's O.K. Have a good evening."

"You too, Miss."

"Good night."

He turns and walks away from me as soon as I start my car. I watch him leave. A big man. Limps a little. Someone told me he'd been shot in the right leg during a robbery he foiled. His gray curly hair bounces irregularly with every step. I quickly gun the motor and leave the garage before he's out of sight.

Once I'm out in the street, driving along, I feel relieved. Hunger starts gnawing at my insides. I forgot to eat lunch. The only thing I've eaten all day has been vending machine peanuts with lukewarm coffee. I really don't feel like going home to my empty apartment. Besides, my cupboards are bare. And I don't feel like cooking just for one person anyway.

The Pines of Rome Restaurant on Connecticut Avenue is on my way home. It has the best vegetable lasagna I've ever tasted. I stop there and go for some takeout. It takes a while for the food to be ready, since it's made to order. I order a diet cola, and take a seat at the table in front while waiting for my food. I idly glance around.

The place is softly lit, fairly empty. There are four or five red carnations in a vase on each table. The white tablecloths shimmer under the light of the candles. I think of Peter. I wish I could hear his low-pitched voice relating anecdotes of his days in the District Attorney's office. Looking at me. Smiling at me.

Ten or twelve customers are dining in the restaurant. Mostly couples. One family with two small children are eating from a large spaghetti plate. They seem very happy. I notice a couple sitting at a corner table, the farthest from the entrance. They are conspicuous, mostly because of their gestures. He's middle-aged, not bad-looking. She's a stunning young woman, probably not much older than my twenty-seven years, with olive skin that seems to glow even in the dim light of the restaurant. Her long, glossy dark hair is tied demurely with a ribbon at the nape of her neck. She's wearing a simple beige linen suit. She is absolutely stunning. She's so beautiful that I can't help staring openly at her. The man seems enraptured by her. Suddenly she starts crying. He leans over to her to dab her eyes very tenderly. I think I recognize the man. I know that face. I just can't place him.

My lasagna arrives. I pay and turn around one more time to look at the couple in the corner. The man must have felt my gaze because he turns around to look at me. I realize it's Robert Verona, Mr. Halifax's driver. But who is that gorgeous woman with him?

On my way home I turn on the radio. Manny is on. He sounds melancholy, infinitely sad: "And now the next love song goes to Linda, with all the love in the world from Robert. Yes, Robert, give her all your love."

That voice. What a beautiful voice.

I eat dinner alone in my empty apartment and wait for Peter to call. A CD of Heifetz playing Saint-Saens' *Rondo Capriccioso* is on. I loved listening to that music when my father played it on his old violin. I would run to get my tambourine and dance like a whirling dervish, round and round, banging on the tambourine. The same sounds that had created in me the image of a happy gypsy are now the unmistakable whimpers of a woman's longing. The same tones, the same chords, are now tearing into my heart. I fall into a fitful sleep.

9

The National Cathedral is packed for Vincent Halifax's funeral service. I find a seat between Sue and Tim Elias. Sue looks grim, sobbing occasionally. Her pale skin appears almost translucent. I wonder why she's so devastated.

The Cathedral is filled with flowers, even though the family has requested that money be donated to charity, in lieu of flowers. With their strong aroma and all the people, the atmosphere in the Cathedral is heavy, almost suffocating. An organist is playing *Ave Maria*. I recognize Senators and Congressmen walking down the aisles, shaking hands with the guests, smiling broadly, slapping one another on the back.

Many local artists are here. They seem truly affected by Mr. Halifax's death. A young man sitting behind me is in tears. Between sobs he tells his companion that now, without Mr. Halifax's support, he might have to go back to driving a truck. Mr. Halifax was a patron of the arts, supporting and encouraging struggling young artists. What a loss his death will be to the art world.

At exactly ten o'clock the Reverend Clay Evans starts the short prayers, and a hush falls over the entire majestic Cathedral. The only sounds are the muffled sobs that came from a woman I was later told was Martha, Mr. Halifax's first wife.

Roger Davis, our Ambassador to Great Britain, walks up to the podium to present the eulogy. His slow pace and haggard look reflect the exhaustion of having flown overnight from London to get to the memorial service. He walks stiffly up the steps to the podium and solemny begins to speak.

"Martha, Irma, Patrick, Walter, dear friends. We will sorely miss Vincent Halifax. A man of character, a man who loved life and everything noble and decent about life. He used his good fortune for charitable causes and to promote the young and the talented in all spheres of the arts. We are all poorer now that Vincent has left us. He has left a great void that nothing and nobody will be able to fill."

His eulogy continues for a long time. My mind strays. The *New York Times* carried a long obituary with many of the details of Mr. Halifax's life. Those fit to print, of course. The heat is getting worse. People are fanning themselves with their elegant, engraved service leaflets. I'm entranced by the Halifax family sitting all together in the first row. In the first pew closest to the center aisle is Irma, dressed in a black Armani suit and a very large veiled hat that covers her face. She keeps looking straight ahead. She doesn't turn around.

Walter is sitting to her left. Tanned, tall, dashing in a navy blue suit, a starched white shirt, and sober navy blue tie. He looks very somber. Whenever he turns around, I can see that his eyes are red-rimmed.

Sue points out to me that next to Walter is his mother, Martha. A diminutive woman with white hair tied in a bun at the nape of her neck. She, too, is dressed all in black, with a lace mantilla on her head. Walter's arm is wrapped protectively around her thin shoulders. She appears to be sobbing. Her whole small frame appears to convulse with sobs.

To her left sits her other son, Patrick, and his wife Samantha. Patrick is a surprising sight to me. He doesn't look at all like Walter. He's smaller, heavier, with wispy light hair and dark brown eyes framed by tortoise shell glasses. He wears a little goatee and mustache. He looks much older than Walter, although Sue told me they're only two years apart. Samantha towers over him. She looks big and heavy even when seated. Imposing. She wears her dark hair very short, cut to one side, and her pierced ears sport large square diamonds. From the back her shoulders look like a quarterback's. Patrick and Samantha keep turning around. I notice that Samantha wears absolutely no makeup. There's a rumor that the President, even though not fully recovered, might attend the memorial service, so with every movement behind them, any rustling sound made by a newcomer, both turn their heads to the center aisle. I'm sitting several rows behind them, on the right side. The entire staff of the radio station is supposed to be at the service. We have part-time people filling in for the midday deejay and the news person. I keep looking for

Manny. I haven't seen him all morning and I'm concerned for him. He sounded so depressed on his show last night that I'm worried he might try to do something foolish. I don't see him sitting among the staff.

On our way out, I spot a dry-eyed Robert Verona dressed in a black suit and a black bow tie. He's sitting very close to the beautiful girl I saw with him the previous night in the restaurant. I notice that Sue and the girl exchange quick glances.

"Do you know her?" I ask. "She's so beautiful."

"No, I don't. Come on, let's go. It's too stuffy in here. Let's get out quickly."

"She's a stunner," I press, turning my head to steal a few more glances at her.

"Gloria, are you coming or not?" She tugs at my arm.

"Goodness. I'm coming, I'm coming."

Sue pushes ahead without answering.

Outside the Cathedral, I'm in the line of staff that files in front of the Halifaxes. I shake their hands and murmur words of sympathy; anything I can think of or that I hear the person in front of me say. When I stop in front of Irma, I say, "I'm so sorry, Irma." She looks straight at me, parts her lips to say something and closes them again without uttering a sound. She's extremely pale. Her hand is cold and clammy. Her stare is very cold.

"Gloria, we're going to Café Milano for lunch. You want to join us?" Sue's voice has taken a gentler tone. She's with a middle-aged man I've never seen before. She introduces him.

"This is Mario Ruiz, general manager of KMEX, Halifax's station in Los Angeles."

I shake Mario's hand. A strong, warm handshake. Five feet ten and round all over. Dark hair, dark eyes, a small mustache. He's wearing a tan suit with a shirt open at the collar.

"Hi, Gloria," he says. "Sue has told me great things about you. Please join us."

"Are you sure I won't be intruding?" I ask. I really want to go with them, I've been feeling so lonely.

"Come along," Sue says. "A few of us are meeting there. We just don't want to go back to the station quite yet. It's depressing over there. You still have a couple of hours before your shift. Come on, join us."

"Great. I'll meet you there. I have to get my car." What I really want to do is stay around a little longer and look around for Manny. There are throngs of people streaming out of the wide doors of the Cathedral. From where I'm standing, it looks like a black sea of people. I can't find Manny.

The day has turned colder. A bracing fall wind is whipping the branches of the trees. Gold and orange leaves are landing softly by my feet. They crunch when I step on them. I love the cool crispness of a Washington fall, even when, like now, the wind stings my face and makes my ears ache. I close my wool jacket up to my chin and start walking quickly behind the National Cathedral School where I parked my car. A man is leaning against the car parked next to mine. He seems vaguely familiar. I can't place him. His hands are stuck into his long brown coat that covers most of his six foot frame. His short black hair is combed neatly, despite the gusty wind. He's puffing on a cigarette. As I approach my car, he straightens up, looks at me, takes out the cigarette form his mouth and exhales the smoke. He smiles. I notice that his teeth are crooked and badly stained. I avert my eyes and start fiddling with my car keys. I'm having trouble putting the car key into the keyhole. I don't know if it's smart to get into my car now. *What if he forces himself into the car with me? What if this is the crazy caller?*

"You're Gloria Berk, right"? He interrupts my thoughts. I don't think I recognize the voice, even though I'm listening intently. I hesitate a few seconds by the open door of my car.

"Um. . .Um. . . Yes, I am."

"I know you from the last remote you did to benefit the Children's Hospital last month. You did a very good job. It was a pleasure seeing you perform in front of all the children. They all seem to love you. You're very good at what you do."

"Thank you very much." I'm starting to warm up to this man.

"I like your show. I listen to your contest a lot. It's a lot of fun. I hope I can get through to the phones one of these days. I'd like to win some of that money."

I relax a bit. I'm becoming paranoid. "Thank you for listening. Please keep trying. I'm sure you'll be able to get through soon." He smiles and we say goodbye.

By twelve o'clock the Café Milano is already very crowded and I can't find my people. Suddenly I see Sue waving at me. There's a chair saved for me next to Sue and across the table from Mario and Tim Elias.

"Mario's telling us stories about Mr. Halifax and Irma," Sue explains. "We ordered salad and lobster ravioli for everybody. I hope you don't mind."

"Sounds great." I sit down and the waiter pours me a glass of white wine.

"Go on, Mario. Give us the whole scoop," Tim says.

"Well. . ." Mario wipes his thick lips with the peach-colored linen napkin, "this is just common knowledge around the station. You see, Irma was working at my station when Halifax met her."

"What did she do there?" I ask.

"She was the receptionist. She was born in Mexico. Her aunt, Emma Perez, worked in our sales department. She invited Irma to come live with her. She thought Irma would have better opportunities here."

"Little did she know how much better," Sue says.

Mario looks at her and smiles. "We found out that Irma's mother was a cleaning lady in one of the big hotels in Mexico City, the Maria Isabel, I think, and she was knocked up by an American guy staying at the hotel. She claimed she had been raped. She was immediately fired from the hotel. Things happen, I guess. Irma was raised by her mother. Irma grew up with huge ambitions–she wanted to be a model, and actress–but her mother had no money to provide her with anything. So when she was seventeen she left Mexico and came to L.A. to live with her aunt and seek a better life."

"Good move," I say. My lobster ravioli is fabulous. I'm

enjoying it tremendously. The waiter pours another glass of white wine.

"She worked for us with no papers," Mario continues. "No I.D. whatsoever. We were breaking the law and Mr. Halifax knew it, but he didn't seem to mind. As a matter of fact, he didn't seem to mind whatever trouble Irma got into. When she joined our station, his trips to L.A. increased from maybe once a year to twice a month. His excuse was that we were having some problems with payola and he himself need-ed to help his attorneys investigate the situation." Mario winks at me. "The whole station knew the real reason. He couldn't take his eyes off Irma. And she appeared to pay no attention to him. There she was, an eighteen-year-old girl, with big breasts and tight sweaters spending her entire day reading romance novels and filing her nails while sitting at the reception desk. She hardly looked at him."

"Was Halifax still married then?" I ask.

"Oh, yes. He divorced his first wife three years later in order to marry Irma," Mario says.

"How did she do it?" Tim asks.

"Beats me. We never saw them leave the station together. We never saw them come in together. And Emma, her aunt, never said a word about their love affair."

"She must've ensnared him," Tim says. "Told him she was pregnant or something."

"I don't think so," Mario answers. "Rumor has it that Mr. Halifax suffered a childhood disease that left him sterile."

Sue and I exchange quick glances. I think that Mario noticed it but didn't react.

"But he has two sons," Tim says.

"Supposedly they're adopted," Mario answers while taking another forkful of ravioli.

"No wonder they look so different," I say.

"To this day I don't understand why he left Mrs. Halifax and married Irma," Mario says after a big gulp of wine. "He brought Mrs. Halifax the first from England, you know. A very fine lady. Very fine. Breaks my heart every time I think that he left her alone. Sweet lady. Had me to her house once when I came for a budget meeting. Great lady."

"Well, I think he still loved his first wife, even to the end," Sue says. "He went by her house every day after work. He stopped at her place to join her in a drink before dinner. I know because I've been called for after-hour meetings and they always took place at old Mrs. Halifax's house. He was always so solicitous of her, filling her glass, holding her hand. It was very sweet."

"That's really odd," I say.

Sue grins widely. "What's really odd," she says "is that when he traveled abroad, no matter where he went or for how long, he took both women along. Both the new and the old Mrs. Halifax went along."

"You're kidding." I honestly think she must be kidding.

"God's truth." She holds up two fingers like a scout.

"I wonder how Irma felt about all this," I ask, mopping up the ravioli sauce with a piece of crusty bread.

"Apparently Irma hates Martha," Mario says. "She refers to her as 'the old cow' because, as she points out, her breasts are so droopy."

"That's not kind." Tim says looking at each one of us. "I didn't think Irma was that mean. Self-centered, showy, flirty, yes. But not mean."

"She hates Martha Halifax," Mario says. "And it doesn't help matters that Halifax let it be known that if he and Irma ever got divorced, Martha would get the bulk of his estate. Irma complained bitterly about this."

Tim lets out a soft, long whisper. "What a weird arrangement."

"Well, Halifax wanted to have it all–and he almost did." Sue gets up, grabs her large shoulder bag. "I'd better be heading back to the station. I must have a thousand calls to return. Come on, kiddo, your shift is going to start soon. Tim, please take care of the bill. Ask Veronica to reimburse you from petty cash when you get back to the station. Leave a nice big tip."

I take a last sip of my wine and shake Mario's hand. "It was a real pleasure. I mean it."

"Same here. Come visit us in L.A. someday. I'll take you to Hollywood. Make you a star."

I giggle. Sue and I dash out. It has been a really interesting lunch.

Manny hasn't shown up to prepare for his show. This has never happened before. Drew Kravitz, the program director, is very upset, running up and down the halls of the station. He bursts into the studio at five forty-five and screams, "Have you seen Manny? Have you heard from him?"

"I'm on the air Drew, please."

I'm worried about Manny. No, I haven't seen him all day.

And no, I haven't heard from him. Drew asks me to take over for Manny for a few minutes while he finds one of Manny's "best of" tapes. Then he apologizes for the distraction and gently closes the doors to the studio.

I put on a CD and dial Manny's phone number. It rings until the machine picks up.

"Hi." The voice, the alluring voice. "This is Manny Miranda. I'm out probably saving the world. Please leave your name and phone number. I really want to know who called. I'll call you back as soon as I can. Bye." *Click.*

At six-thirty I'm on my way home exhausted from this day. The first thing I do when I walk in my door is to call Manny again. Still not picking up. I brew a cup of strong coffee, open my Criminal Law book, prop my feet on the coffee table and start studying for tomorrow's class.

The phone is ringing. I hear it coming from very far away. It wakes me up. I look at the clock on the mantlepiece above my gas fireplace. It's twelve-thirty a.m. All the lights in the apartment are on and my book is open on my lap to the first case I started to read.

"Yes?" I answer hoarsely.

"Gloria, it's Peter. Sorry I woke you."

Sweet God, thank you. Thank you, God. He's calling me. Maybe he wants to come over now.

I sit up straight and murmur, "Peter . . . Would you . . ."

He interrupts me sharply. "Gloria, listen. Listen to me. I just came back from a meeting with an assistant D.A., a former student of mine. I wanted to discuss Manny's problem with him. He told me Manny's been arrested for the murder of Vincent Halifax. He needs help."

10

"Why, Peter, why?" My voice is too shrill. "I know Manny couldn't have done it. He's a very good and very kind person. He couldn't have killed anybody, much less Mr. Halifax."

We're sitting at Max's Bar and Grill on Columbia Road, just two blocks from my apartment. It's open till five in the morning. I'm nursing a hot toddy and Peter is drinking a beer. When he heard how upset I was about Manny's arrest, he suggested we get together. I invited him to come up to my apartment but he chose Max's Bar and Grill instead. I guess he's trying to tell me something.

I threw on a sweatsuit and sprinted over to the bar. When I walked in, he was already sitting at a corner table. It's a very small place and quite dark. It's almost deserted at one a.m. Only two other people are here, playing chess, smoking, and drinking something.

Peter looks so good to me. He's wearing a navy blue turtleneck, a denim jacket and faded jeans. He smiled broadly at me when I came in. My heart jumped when I saw that friendly, welcoming smile. *Oh Peter, Peter. If I could just run over to you, hug you tightly and kiss those wonderful lips.* Instead, I just sat down next to him and squeezed his hand. It's so late now and his blue eyes look very tired.

"I know you don't believe he could have done it," he says. He's stroking my hand lightly. "You like him too much, he's a good friend, you work together. It's hard to imagine that someone you think you know well could murder anyone."

I'm shaking my head all the while he's talking. "Peter, I know he didn't do it." I'm adamant.

"How do you know this, babe?" he asks gently.

B*abe, he called me babe. I adore this man.*

"I just know." I sound like a total imbecile.

"Gloria, the police have a lot of evidence against him." He's suddenly very serious. I'm petrified.

"What kind of evidence?"

"The weapon that killed Mr. Halifax has been identified as Manny's, for starters."

"What weapon? How was he killed?" I don't want to know. I'm afraid to hear the details. I don't even like to look at blood.

"He was stabbed in the heart with a dagger."

I feel faint. I hold on to the table to steady myself. "A dagger? What do you mean a dagger?"

"A silver dagger that was identified as Manny's."

"Who identified it?"

"Several people, Gloria."

"Like who?" I'm very belligerent now.

"Several people at the station. They've told the police that they've seen him toying with the dagger at the station."

"Peter," I'm holding my breath, "is it silver with a malachite holder?" I suddenly feel very relieved.

"Yes. So you've seen it too."

"For goodness sake, that's not a dagger, it's a letter opener. A silver letter opener. Manny always keeps it at his desk. His parents gave it to him when he graduated from college. He loves that thing. He cherishes it. He's always polishing it. Even when he's sitting talking to you he's polishing it. Everybody at the station knows he has it. It's a letter opener, not a weapon. I can tell them that."

"It was plunged into Mr. Halifax's heart. It was the murder weapon and it has Manny's fingerprints all over it." Peter sounds grim. "And he had a motive. He told several people that nobody was going to embarrass him again the way he was embarrassed at the station the day of the staff meeting. That he would see to it that it would never happen again."

"That doesn't mean he killed Mr. Halifax," I say. "He'd have to be crazy to use that letter opener. Everybody knows it's his."

"Murderers do crazy things. People heard him making threats, Gloria. The police and the District Attorney always take threats seriously. And Manny was very vocal about it."

"He didn't mean anything by it." As though I could tell what Manny meant or didn't mean.

"There's more, babe. The police found his fingerprints in the Halifax residence."

"Of course there would be prints there. He's been there. I saw him there only last week. My prints are there too. Are they going to arrest me too?"

"Gloria, calm down. There were fresh fingerprints on a glass that had been washed that afternoon."

"How do they know that?" I'm getting sadder by the minute.

"The maid told the police she had washed all the crystal the afternoon of the murder and had put it away. No other glasses with fingerprints other than hers were found. He was at the estate the day of the murder and it's his dagger that killed Halifax. That doesn't prove he killed Halifax, but it is pretty solid evidence."

"It is not a dagger, it's a letter opener." *When will I learn to keep my mouth shut.*

He touches my chin briefly. "I realize you're upset," he says. "If you want to help your friend, I can look for a good criminal attorney to take his case. If Manny wants me to, of course."

"Thank you, Peter." I'm starting to calm down. "I appreciate your help. And thanks for meeting me so late. I mean, it's almost two-thirty. Won't your wife be upset you're not home?" *There, I said it. I broached the subject.* I gear myself up for the answer.

"I don't have a wife, Gloria." *Thank you again, God, thank you.* "My wife died five years ago. She was very ill for several years." *Oh, God, please let me die now—always putting my foot in my mouth.*

"I'm so sorry. I had no idea."

He takes my hand. "Don't worry, Gloria. There's no reason you would've known. It's not something I talk about a lot. I thought that maybe you should know now."

Why, I'm wondering, *why should I know? Does he want me? Does he find me attractive? Maybe I can invite him up to my apartment now.* I'm aching to hold him close to me. My skin is burning with desire. My palms are moist and my mouth is dry.

I take a sip of my drink. "Would you like to. . . have dinner with me tomorrow night?" Tonight is not the right time to start an affair with this man. "I'm a pretty good cook. Everything I know I learned from my mother, the world's best cook, according to my father." *Please say yes.*

He smiles at my little family recommendation. "Tomorrow night I teach," he says. "You have a class with me, in case you forgot." He's smiling that wonderful smile. "But Friday would be very nice, if the invitation's still open."

We walk together the two blocks to my apartment. He has his hands in the pockets of his jeans. I slide my arm through his. He squeezes it. I can hardly breathe.

The day at the station has been uneventful. Everybody has heard about Manny's arrest but nobody is talking about it. At least not that I can hear. We tiptoe past the coffee machine and whisper when we walked into the studio. Nobody seems to want to get together in the staff lounge and chat as we always do. We're all immersed in our thoughts, reacting to our common tragedy in total disbelief.

This very afternoon, Drew Kravitz, the program director, has started a nation-wide search for Manny's replacement. We're in the midst of a ratings period and could lose a lot of listeners in Manny's time period if we just play CD's or Manny's old tapes. It's the combination of his ad libs, his charming raunchy humor, wonderful voice, and the dedications that make Manny's program so popular. Drew doesn't want to lose all those loyal listeners. It will be very hard to get them back, even if Manny returns to his slot soon—and who knows when that might be? And anyway, even if he were released on bond, what are the chances he'd be allowed to return to work at the station? After all, he is accused of murdering the owner of the radio station. Somehow, Manny being on the air while he's considered the murderer is out of the question. Drew wants another Silver Fox, and he wants him now.

"I just don't think that's fair," I say to Drew. "After all, Manny's almost certainly innocent and he'll want his job back. And if you do take him back, it won't be fair to fire the person you've hired to replace him."

"I know all you're saying is right, Gloria. I'm just following orders."

"But you're the program director. You decide on all the programming staff. You decide who gets hired and who gets fired. Don't you?"

He turns away from me. His big glasses emphasize his narrow forehead and his long nose. "I'm just following orders," he repeats woodenly.

"Whose orders, may I ask?"

"Mrs. Halifax's," he answers somberly.

I have to do something to help Manny. I know that the police have it all wrong. Manny's innocent. And I'm going to prove it. Where do I start? What do I do? I have to believe he's innocent. Manny, my sweet friend Manny. I know the whole story of his family and his ambitions. He has a real sense of the value of human lives. He's told me about his close-knit family. He talks about his parents, Jose and Maria, with tears of pride in his eyes. Both were born near Cuernavaca, Mexico, children of poor farmers. They came from large families, struggling merely to survive. Manny's father was already married to Maria when he left Mexico. He was twenty-one. He got to the border and was helped across by Maria's family, who lived in San Diego. He worked for five years as a migrant worker before he was able to send for his bride. They settled in a small room in an apartment occupied by two other families in a Hispanic section of L.A., and that's where Manny and his two younger sisters were born. His mother is a day maid and his father is a gardener in Beverly Hills. It's a story like many others, but to Manny it's his life. Manny always speaks of his parents with great emotion. It's obvious he loves them very deeply.

Manny worked in a supermarket as a bag boy to help out his parents. In high school and college he took any position he could get at radio stations. He always loved radio. When he graduated from college he went into it full-time. He told me that the day he graduated from college was the proudest moment for his family. It meant so much to all of them. Now he's helping his youngest sister go to college to become an architect. His parents have been able to move to a nicer neighborhood with his financial help, and they have a three bedroom apartment—with one of the bedrooms set aside as his, for his occasional visits. His mother still works as a cleaning woman, but now it's only two days a week. Manny affectionately calls her "his lady of leisure."

His mother was the one who gave him the letter opener. It was his graduation present.

He has also been good and gentle to me. Last year, when my parents moved away, I was terribly lonely. I was moping around half the time. Only Manny seemed to notice my sadness and, in his kind manner, would sometimes keep me company if he wasn't working evenings or on long week ends, no matter what else he needed to do. He wouldn't leave my side until he had made me laugh and promise him that all was well in my little world. Sweet, sweet Manny.

He's got to be going crazy now, sitting in jail, brooding, accused of murdering a wealthy, powerful man. I hope with all my heart that he's been wrongly accused.

After a lackluster shift, I'm ready to go to Peter's class. I'm unprepared again. I have to catch up with my studies or I'll surely flunk the course. *My God, what would Peter think of me then? And what would my parents say?* This weekend I intend to spend every free moment studying. I'll read every case, memorize every rule.

Drew has decided to replace Manny temporarily with a part-time deejay. Big mistake. Part-timers are not very good and not very reliable. Well, he's the program director. I guess he must know what he's doing. I'm just sorry that Manny's audience will disappear by the time he gets back to his shift. Whenever that is. I put on my jacket and tie my scarf around my neck. If I hurry, I can read over one or two cases before class starts.

I'm on my way out. I'm the only one left here other than the new part-timer. No one is in the reception hall and the desktop is clean. Veronica is very good about tidying up her desk before she leaves for the evening. I bend down to leave her a funny little note on her desk. Sometimes I leave a chocolate bar or a piece of candy. She likes to find them there when she comes in in the morning. As I'm writing, the reception phone rings. I really don't want to answer it. It's going to make me late. It seems very insistent and I can't resist. I pick it up and answer brusquely: "WVVV, can I help you?"

There's a pause on the other side.

"Hello, hello," I say. "Is anybody there? This is WVVV." I'm about to hang up. "This is not funny, you know." I can hear breathing at the other end and I'm curious so I don't hang up.

"Missy . . ." a heavily Spanish-accented voice says, "Missy Gloria?" It's a woman's soft voice.

"Yes . . ."

"Missy, this is Lucia Toledo."

I have no idea who that is.

"Lucia Toledo, Mr. Halifax maid." Oh yes, now I remember. I chatted with her for a few minutes during the Halifax cocktail party when she was passing around hors d'oeuvres. She seemed embarrassed by my attention but glad that someone had noticed her. "Is good I find you still at the station. I not know your home phone. I want to call you there."

"Yes, Lucia, what can I do for you?" *Oh God, I'm going to be late to class again. What a wonderful impression I'm making on Peter.*

Hesitation. Long, long pause.

"Lucia, is there a problem? Are you in some sort of danger? Can I help you in any way?"

"No Missy, just that. . . I find something. I want you to see it. I want give it to you."

"What is it, Lucia? Is it important?"

"I think very important. For Manny. You come, Missy. I show you. You come now. I am alone."

"Where are you?" *Good grief, there goes my class.*

"Halifax residence. Nobody home. Come soon, please." She hangs up.

11

I'm driving like a fiend down Wisconsin Avenue to get to Peter before class starts. Stores are still open–they stay open late on Thursday nights, and there are lots of shoppers on the sidewalks. I don't remember when I last went shopping. This murder has turned my life upside down. I can't believe I am hurrying to get to the Halifax estate for a clandestine meeting. I hope I can convince Peter to accompany me. I'm afraid to touch anything there or do anything that might hurt Manny's case. The traffic is murder. I could get there faster if I walked. I finally arrive at the campus at six forty-five. I have to leave the car running in front of the entrance to the law school and sprint in to talk to Peter before class starts.

He's already at the podium, at his desk, shuffling and arranging papers which he never uses anyway during his class. He doesn't even look at them while he lectures. I guess he uses them only as props. His classes are in the Socratic method; he peppers us with questions and tries to make us come up with the correct deductions. At the end, there is always his brief discourse on civil rights or whatever pet project he may have at the time. Great class.

"Peter." I'm breathless. "Come with me. Cancel class. We may be able to help Manny." I tell him what Lucia said. "She says I've got to get it right now. Peter, please come."

He looks at me sternly. "Get a hold of yourself. You know that I can't cancel my class. People here are paying good money to hear me lecture. Wait for me after class and then we can go together."

"No, Peter. I can't do that. She said to go there immediately while no one else is there. I really have to go. I'm just afraid to disturb anything." I'm almost in tears. I want his support.

"Go there," he says more kindly. "Just make sure that you don't touch anything. Take whatever the maid has for you, and after class I'll meet you at your apartment so we can look over what she gives you."

My apartment! That sounds very good. Very promising. "O.K." I say. "I'm really sorry I miss your class again. I love it. You know that." I'm apologizing and I truly mean it.

"I know, Gloria. Now go. Drive safely. Don't disturb anything at the house. I'll see you at your place around ten-thirty or so. I'll bring us something to eat."

Peter, I just adore you. "Thank's, Peter! Have a good class. I'll see you soon." I run up the steps to the door of the small auditorium and bump into Steve. Actually bump into his strong, hard body. He holds me by my arms, quite close to him, and smiles.

"Whoa, Gloria. What's the rush? Is the school burning down?"

"No, no Steve." I'm not moving away. *What a nice masculine grip he has. Smells good, too.* "There's an emergency at the radio station that I have to take care of," I lie. *Since when did I become such an accomplished liar?* "I really have to run."

"Can I help? Do you need some police protection?" He winks at me.

"Not tonight. Not really. Very nice of you to ask." He's still holding on to me. I look back at the podium and notice that Peter is watching us. I feel myself blush. But still, I don't pull away from Steve. I never noticed how broad his chin is and how blue his eyes are.

"Can we have a drink sometime? I promise I'll behave."

"I'd like that. Maybe next week. I really have to go now."

"I'll hold you to your promise." He brushes the hair off my forehead and straightens out my scarf. "Behave, now. . ."

"Sure. Thank you," and I rush into the cold street for my drive to Potomac. I know the way very well. My parents lived there for a long time. It's where I was born and raised. I saw it transformed from a sleepy little Maryland suburb–the Village, as we used to call it, where we all knew each other, with horses prancing behind the white Potomac fences–to a majestic neighborhood with million-dollar estates. It was good my parents moved away. They wouldn't like their old digs much now. They're simple folk, or so they claim.

The George Washington Parkway is a mess. I change

lanes, speed past one car and then another. Cars are honking all around me and I don't seem to be making much progress.

Finally, I take a turn onto River Road and emerge in Halifax's neighborhood. My old neighborhood. It brings back sweet memories of my childhood, of music and hugs and love and good food.

The Halifax mansion, at last. The enormous house is very dark, except for one lit room off the garage. I assume that's Lucia's room. The chill of the night air makes me shiver as I get out of the car. It's dark and cold outside. The house looks so different today than it did just last week, during the cocktail party. Now it looks gloomy, forbidding. Oppressive, really. It's very quiet around here. Just some cricket and frog calls. I haven't heard those sounds since I moved to the city. I had forgotten how wonderful the sounds of nature are. The garden lights are suddenly turned on and I see that the house is surrounded by very tall trees - they look like pines or spruces. Planted close to the house are tall grasses that sway gracefully in this blustery evening. It's an interesting garden. Very natural. I hear a dog bark from a far.

I climb the two wide stone steps to the entrance. I hadn't noticed before that the two columns at either side of the entrance are made from very fine polished stone. They look like Carrara marble. They reflect the garden lights. Grandiose. The stained glass doors are somber; the glorious amber and gold colors I saw last week seem to have vanished without the backlighting from inside. I hesitate at the door. I don't know if I should ring the bell. I hear shuffling steps coming close to the door and then I see the door open a bit. There's only the faintest light inside.

Lucia slips outside. She gives me a stern, cold look.

My slight frame towers over her five feet. Her dark lined face, small eyes and broad nose remind me of an Aztec sculpture. She's wearing black, with a knit shawl wrapped around her.

"Missy, I thought you not coming no more," she says. "I call you long ago." She sounds very annoyed. She's not happy with me.

"Lucia, I'm sorry. The radio station is very far away from here. What is it that you found? What did you find for me?" I'm speaking very brusquely. I don't like standing here. I don't like the darkness and the remoteness of the place. Let me be back in my own cozy apartment with Peter at my side. It's obvious she's not going to let me in.

"This is what I found, Missy." She produces a small black book from under her shawl. It must be five by seven inches. It's bound in shiny leather and the sides of the pages are rimmed in gold.

"What is this, Lucia? Where did you find it?" I'm afraid to even touch the book.

She looks down and shuffles her slipper-clad feet. She looks embarrassed. She hesitates and stammers when she answers: "I find in one of the Mrs. drawers."

"Mrs. Halifax's drawers?"

"Yes."

"Irma Halifax's drawers?"

"Yes."

Oh, my God. What am I doing with something that belongs

to Irma? How can this help Manny? What can happen to me? What do I do? Do I take it or run?

"Lucia, why did you take this?"

"It help Mr. Manny."

"How do you know it will help Manny?"

"You read it. You see." She shoves the book into my hand and is ready to go back in.

"Lucia, wait. Do the police know about this?"

"No. Nobody know anything about it."

"Why are you giving this to me?" I am genuinely curious.

"You are friend of Mr. Manny. He like you."

"How do you know this, Lucia?" I ask, incredulous.

"He tell me so." *How come Manny tells this woman he likes me?*

"How does he tell you? When did he tell you?"
She looks at me as though she's looking at a twelve-year-old innocent child.

"Manny is son of my cousin Maria. He take me to Church in Washington every Sunday morning. We talk. He good boy. He not kill Mr. Halifax. I listen to him every night in my little radio. He good in radio."

"Lucia, did you tell any of this to the police? To anybody else?"

"Nobody ask me this. They ask me very little. They only ask if I here the night of murder and I say no. I not here. I in church. Every Monday night I walk to church near here to serve dinner to poor people. I am in church the night of murder." I look at her with great admiration. She goes out of her way to help others. I had better do the same.

"Was anybody else at home that night, before you left for Church?"

"When I go at five in the evening the only person here is Mr. Halifax. He not feeling well that evening. The Mrs. is at the station, like every day now. Mr. Walter in his gallery, they have party there."

"What about Robert, the driver?"

"I not know where Señor Verona was. He has apartment here, above the garage. Up there, second floor." She points upward. "He live there. I not see from my room when he come in or go out." A cold wind is picking up. Lucia shudders and wraps her shawl more tightly around her. "You read book, Missy. You bring back. You help Manny. He very good boy. He no kill nobody." She puts the small book in my hand, then takes hold of my other hand in both of hers. Her hands are very small, rough, and cold. "God bless you, Missy. Please help my Manny." She turns around and walks into the dark, quiet house.

The small book seems to be burning a hole in the pocket of my jacket. I'm dying to start reading it. But I want to share it with Peter. It makes me think that somehow, it will bring us together, that it's romantic in a way. I lay the black leather book next to me in the car, under my leg. The traffic going back to Washington is much lighter. I zoom down the parkway. When I get to Connecticut Avenue I stop at a liquor store. I take the book with me, hold it close to my chest as I buy a bottle of red wine, a bottle of port, and a six-pack of beer for Peter.

At home I turn the lights on and place the book in the middle of the glass coffee table. After putting the beer in the refrigerator, I decide to light a fire. It's a gas fireplace with artificial logs. It doesn't make the crackling noise of a wood fire. It doesn't give out too much warmth either, but its flames bathe the living room in a soft amber glow. It's quite a romantic fire.

I sit and do nothing, waiting for Peter. My eyes are riveted on the book.

When he knocks, I run to the door, open it and just stare at him. He looks so good standing there smiling, arms loaded with containers of food. I'm just holding the door open.

"Well," he says "aren't you going to let me in?" He pushes the door gently with his shoulder, walks past me right into the tiny kitchen and puts all the containers of food on the white Formica counter. He's been here for no more than two minutes and he looks as though he owns the place.

"So, what did you get?" he asks while opening the containers.

"I'll show you in a second. First, do you want beer or red wine?"

"Let me start with a cold beer. I'm very thirsty." The kitchen is so small that I have to squeeze behind him to get to the refrigerator. I hand him a beer. He holds my wrist with one hand and grasps the beer with the other. If only I had the guts to put my arms around him and hold him close to me. Ah, to feel his entire body pressed to mine that night when I made a fool of myself and he had to put me to bed. I've never mentioned that night to him. He hasn't either. But I'd like to ask him what he thought of what he saw. I don't dare. He releases my hand, takes a gulp of beer and says, "Well, talk to me, lady. What did you find out? What was so important you had to miss my great class?" He smiles. How I love that smile.

We're standing very close to each other. Neither of us moves away.

"I have a book that the maid found in Irma's dresser."

"A book!" He sounds very disappointed. He turns to the food. He serves two heaping dishes of *pad thai*. "I hope you like Thai food," he says as he mixes the noodles and the vegetables and squeezes a few drops of lemon on it. "It's vegetarian. Lots of tofu. And a little spicy. It's good for you."

I take a taste with my fingers. "It's very good."

"Well, Gloria," he says. "Are you going to tell me about the book or do you want me to guess"? He starts walking with both plates in his hands toward the small dining room table. I follow him with two glasses and the bottle of wine.

"I haven't looked at it. I thought we could do it together."

"Well, bring it over to the table. Let's look at it while we eat. By the way, it's very hot in here, do you mind very much turning down the fire a little?" *There goes my romantic idea of the fire.*

We sit next to each other at the table facing the small balcony. My leg is touching his. He's gobbling down his food. I'm mostly staring at him.

"By the way," he asks between mouthfuls, "do you and Steve Palmer have anything . . . ?

"Oh, no, no," I answer much too quickly. "We're only

classmates." I'm happy he noticed.

"I see."

I place the book on the table, between the two of us and open it gingerly. "Oh, my God, Peter. It's a diary. Do you think we ought to read it? I feel weird doing this."

"We might as well since it's already here."

"Would you like to read it now?" I ask.

"I can't see it too well in this dim light. Why don't you read it aloud so we can both hear it at the same time."

He leans back in his chair, takes the glass of wine in one hand and wraps the other arm around my chair. I can feel the tips of his fingers softly grazing my bare arm.

12

"July 18," I begin, reading aloud. "Vince is out of town. Again. I think he's in New York. He's been going to New York very often lately. I'm always alone in this house. The maid is out and so is the chauffeur. I can hear Walter upstairs in his quarters playing loud music. Some rock. I wonder if he has any friends visiting him there. Or maybe a woman. I haven't seen him with a woman in a while. I've been looking at Walter lately. I don't think I ever really looked at him before. He's really not bad looking at all. Has good height, a nice body. I like his muscular legs. Tanned, covered with golden hairs. I think he caught me looking at him yesterday, when he went swimming. Vince may also have seen me looking at him.

"I just don't get enough sex from Vince. It's not like it used to be three years ago. That's when things changed. I'm starved for sex. I need it. I dream of it. I walk around all day long thinking about it. And I'm so alone in this big house.

"I think I'll go see what Walter is doing. Maybe we can have a drink together. Listen to some music together. I need to feel a body close to me."

I pause. I look at Peter. He's sitting very still, with his eyes half closed.

"Are you listening?" I ask.

"I'm listening. Go on."

"Do you think this could help Manny in any way?"

"I don't know yet, Gloria. Let's continue."

My mouth is very dry. I would like to cuddle against Peter's arm and feel his body against mine. I can feel his warmth next to me. I take a sip of wine, move my chair a little closer to his. His breath caresses my neck. I shudder a bit and continue:

"July 22. I went out to eat with my friends tonight. It was quite good. I insisted Vince come along and join us. He did. Reluctantly. He never seems to be at ease with my friends. Maybe because they're all so much younger than him. Maybe because he just doesn't want to be bothered. He was quiet and moody all evening. He made everybody feel he would have preferred not to be there. To my left was Philip, my dermatologist. Nice man, but too bland for me. Too pale. Too quiet. He was boring me. I decided to have a little fun. When the conversation started to lag a bit during the main course I let my left hand slide down, I put it on my lap under the table cloth and I moved it slowly until I placed it on Philip's thigh. He didn't move. He didn't react at all. I let it rest there for a while and continued chatting away about my dance class. He didn't move a muscle. His fork just hung there, in mid-air. I slid it a little bit higher. He was as stiff as a board. He didn't even turn to me. He didn't look at me. Just continued staring straight ahead. I wanted to laugh out loud. I looked at him and smiled. He still didn't look at me. Patricia, his wife, was sitting on his other side. I leaned over my plate, to speak to Patricia, right in front of Philip. I asked her how her bridge game was coming along. When she started to answer me, I grabbed Philip's crotch. Just left my hand there. He jumped and uttered a very small cry. He sounded like a cat. Everybody asked him what happened. He said a fish bone had gotten stuck in his throat. What fun. I think Vince may have noticed where my hand had been. He was very quiet on the way home. Never mentioned the incident, though.

"I looked for Walter when we returned. See if he wanted to have a night cap. He wasn't home. I've got to find out who he's seeing now."

I let out an embarrassed laugh. "Some fun," I say. "Can you believe it?"

"I guess Vincent Halifax knew what he was marrying."

"Anything here that can help Manny?" I just want to stop for a while to hear what Peter's thinking. How he's reacting to these words. To listen to his voice close to my ear. To feel his breath upon my skin.

"I haven't heard anything of any help to him yet. Do you feel comfortable reading this out loud?" he asks.

How do I answer that question? If I say "yes," I'm a shame-less, hussy. If I say "no," I'm a prude.

"If you feel all right with my reading it, I don't mind going on."

"I'm fine with it. I like the sound of your voice very much."

My heart took a tumble. *I'm reading him this private quasi-pornographic diary and he's listening to the sound of my voice.* I'm getting quite excited by the words I'm reading, by Peter's close proximity, and by my thoughts about Peter. I just hope he doesn't notice it in the tone of my voice. I read on.

"July 27. Vincent hasn't touched me in over a month. We sleep in the same room, in the same bed, and I have a stranger by my side. A stranger might not be a bad idea. I wouldn't mind sex with a stranger or even a rebuff from a stranger. But when I put my hand between Vince's legs and he pulls away from it, I'm very hurt.

"Last night when he came home from the office and from visiting his dear ex-wife Martha, I asked him to go downstairs with me to the pool house while I swam before dinner. First he told me he was tired, but when I insisted he finally went with me. He was still wearing his business suit. It was hot and muggy in the poolhouse, but he didn't even take off his jack-et. I mixed him a drink in the pool house bar, turned the lights low, put on the pool lights and took off my robe. I was wear-ing nothing underneath. He hardly looked at me. My body doesn't seem to excite him any more. When we started seeing each other, the mere sight of my naked skin drove him wild.

Tonight, he merely finished his drink and told me he would wait for me for dinner, to hurry up with my swim. When he left the pool house, I kept swimming a bit. When I started up the steps out of the pool I noticed someone was watching. I made believe I didn't notice and didn't cover myself. He kept staring. It was Walter."

Peter's fingers are caressing my arm as I read. I'm wearing a short sleeve pink sweater and my jeans. I've taken my shoes off and my feet are up on another chair. I lean closer to Peter. My head is very close to his cheek. I can feel his breath on my ear. I don't want to move at all. I don't want to move a muscle so that his gentle fingers continue touching my skin.

"Go on," he whispers. "Go on."

"July 29. It's so hot outside. It's just stifling. I can't even walk outside. I hate the summers in Washington. I don't understand why we had to stop going away. We used to go to the South of France for the entire summer. But suddenly it all stopped. These last two summers have been completely horrible. Just because Vincent decided we shouldn't travel so far every year, I must remain here and fry. I hate it here. Thank goodness for Walter's presence. He's been quite attentive lately. He pulls out the chairs for me, opens door for me, smiles at me. Quite the gentleman. Vincent doesn't seem to have noticed the change. I have, though. I have noticed it and I like it. A lot. Last night, before we all retired for bed, I leaned over to kiss Walter on the forehead and he brushed my breast lightly with his fingertips. Sent chills up and down my spine.

121

When I went to bed, Vince was already asleep. I was desperate to feel Walter close to me. I couldn't sleep."

I put the diary down on my lap and turn to look at Peter. "I don't know how this can help Manny much. I don't know if I should keep reading. What're we learning from this? She doesn't even mention Manny."

Peter gives me a tender look. "Suppose there really is an affair between Walter and Irma and suppose Vincent Halifax finds out about it. What if Halifax threatened to cut Walter out of his will and to divorce Irma. Well, you don't need much more than that to forge a powerful motive. Also remember, my dear, that both Irma and Walter had the opportunity to kill, since they both live there. They also both have access to the radio station and both have the means to steal Manny's letter opener and set him up." He takes a sip of wine. "On the other side," he continues, "as I understand it, Walter was at his gallery opening and Irma was at the station, on the air, during your contest. She has millions of witnesses."

"Well, Peter, there are some details that I haven't been able to share with you. Walter apparently arrived very late at the gallery opening—at least an hour and a half after the guests started to arrive. A lot of the people who were there will vouch for that. And Irma was not at the studio when I ran the contest. I imitated her voice. Nobody knew about it, only she and I. And now you."

"Well, well, well." He sits up, smiling. "This is quite an interesting development. Come with me." He takes me by the arm and leads me to the love seat. "Make yourself comfortable, my dear, and continue reading. This story is now taking on a whole new dimension. Let's listen with great care." He pours me another glass of wine, goes to the refrigerator to grab a second beer, and comes jauntily over to the love seat. "Excuse me, my lady, may I sit next to you?" Without waiting for a reply, he sits very close to me. Our legs are propped up on the coffee table, our heads are very close together, my body is touching his and I feel very mellow.

"Go on, babe."

"August 2. Vincent is traveling to New York again. I told him I would go with him and we could go to restaurants and to shows. He said it wasn't a good idea because he would be working very hard and would be too tired to go out at night. So I stayed home. Again. I don't mind it so much now, though. I want to see Walter. I want to be with Walter right now. But I'm afraid that if I walk out of my room into Walter's quarters upstairs Lucia will hear me. She's like Vincent's little spy around here. I don't trust her. She tells him everything. God, I must see Walter tonight. It was so hot this afternoon. So hot. I decided to go swimming. Walter joined me. He was wearing a very tight, very small bathing suit. He was nearly naked. I could see his nakedness very clearly. My eyes were glued to his bathing suit every time he came out of the pool. I didn't even try to conceal my desire. I was drinking a glass of lemonade and just placed the glass between my breasts. He saw that. I'm sure he knows by now how much I want him. He knows I want him to take me. Hard. All night. He could read it in my eyes and in my mouth. We sat together in the spa for a while, with the whirlpool going very strong. My hands were on the inside of my thighs and the bubbles were whirling all around me. I kept caressing my thighs. It was one of the most sensual afternoons I've spent in a long time. But we couldn't even sit close to each other. The gardeners were working near the glass doors of the pool house all afternoon. The chauffeur, that idiot Verona, was hanging around looking at my breasts every chance he had and Lucia was coming and going bringing "snacks" for Señor Walter. I wanted them all out of there, out of my house.

"I've got to see Walter. It's very late now, Vincent isn't here. Lucia, I'm sure, is asleep and I have no idea where Verona might be. I just have to see Walter right now. I'm burning with desire for him. I've got to find a way."

I rest my cheek against Peter's arm. "You want to hear more?" I ask.

"Hmmm," he whispers in my ear. "More." He slides his arm around my shoulder. "More, babe."

I go on.

"August 3. My God. What an exciting, marvelous lover Walter is. I can hardly believe it. Superb. Last night I couldn't wait one more minute. I walked out of my bedroom barefoot, slowly climbed the stairs to his quarters. I felt almost like a thief. I quietly let myself into his bedroom. It was bathed in moonlight. He was lying on the bed, uncovered, completely naked. I stood there for a while and looked at his strong body, so lean, muscular, his long legs half open, his arms spread to each side. I almost think he was waiting for me. I was wearing only a flimsy silk robe. The flesh-colored one Vincent picked out for me for our honeymoon because he said it made me look so young–virginal and sexy. I untied the satin ribbon and let the robe slide down my body to the floor. Walter was lying there, his face half turned to me. I couldn't see his eyes. I didn't know if he had heard me come in. I took a few steps and slid onto the bed next to him. He turned to me immediately and embraced me and kissed me hard. He was pressing his body to mine. He became hard almost instantly. He gently pried my legs open with his knee and penetrated me without uttering a single word. We made love like animals. Without restraint. With no boundaries. It was absolutely delicious. I'm exhausted today. And sore. Vincent is coming back tonight. What will I do? I want more of Walter. I want some of him right now."

Peter's arm had traveled down to my waist. He's holding me tight and I'm nestled in the crook of his arm. I feel very comfortable there. Like I belong there. I feel his lips very softly touching the nape of my neck. *God, make this night last forever.*

"August 15. Walter and I haven't had a moment to be alone since Vincent's return. We've been surrounded by people from morning till night. I'm consumed with desire for Walter. I see him at the morning breakfast table, with his robe half open, and I cannot take my eyes from his strong legs. I want to feel them again around my body. When he leans

125

down to kiss my cheek goodbye I inhale his scent. I want to grasp his hand and put it against my breast. I'm going crazy with desire. I don't know if Vincent has noticed; I can hardly breathe when Walter is close to me.

"Verona has been very smug with me lately. I wonder if he suspects anything. I don't trust him at all. I think he's a snake. A snake with a pock-marked face. I will not let him blackmail me the way he's blackmailing Vincent. I know he's black-mailing him. I'm just positive about it. I found the ledger Vincent keeps hidden in the Statom sculpture in his den. It shows payments Vincent has been making to Verona. I don't know what Verona could have against my husband. I'll con-front that idiot Verona with it if he ever dares to be smart with me.

"There's a charity ball at the Corcoran Gallery tonight. Vincent is on the Board so we all have to put in a command performance. Walter must go too. That's great. I'll be dancing with him tonight. Very close to him. I want to feel his won-derful body pressed to me. I need him so terribly much. I ache for him. My insides are raw for him. I must tell him how great my desire for him is. And I can't be with him. Vincent does-n't have any plans to leave soon. Walter and I must find a way to be together."

I take a deep breath. "That is the last entry," I say. I look expectantly at Peter's lips.

He sits up. "We have to find out more about Verona," he says. "He lives in that house too. He should also be a suspect. And, if Irma is to be believed, he might have had a motive too."

"But how would he have gotten hold of Manny's letter opener?"

"Is Verona at the station sometimes?"

"Once in a while he brings Irma and picks her up. When he does that, he likes to come up and chat with Scott, the Sports Guy."

"Well, that would have given him an opportunity to swipe Manny's letter opener."

"Peter," I whisper and turn toward him. I put my arms around his shoulders and hug him softly. I bury my head in his chest. I inhale his cologne. His sweater is rubbing against my cheek. I can hear the sounds of his heart.

He hugs me back. We stay in each other arms for a long, long time.

"I've got to go, my dear. I've got an early class tomorrow morning. Sleep tight, angel. I'll be seeing you soon." He gently lifts my head by my chin. He kisses me lightly on the lips. Very lightly.

13

It's Friday. Casual day at the station. Not that we need too much prodding for us to be casual. We usually all dress in jeans at the station every day. Except for Sue and Drew Kravitz. And Natalie, the bookkeeper. They never dress in jeans. Not even during casual days. I walk in at noon wearing my jeans and my denim shirt and my tennis shoes. Real casual. I didn't get too much sleep last night but I don't feel tired at all. I'm exhilarated. I know there are other suspects in Mr. Halifax's murder and that Peter's starting to believe that Manny might not be guilty. At least he's not the only one with a motive. That's a gain. Last night I went to bed and reread Irma's diary. Not because of any prurient interest, but rather as a handbook on how to get the man you want. I don't think I learned much.

Sue isn't in her office. It would be good to have a chat

with her just to find out what's happening at the station. I decide to prepare my show very well to have a terrific shift. As I'm about to enter the studio, Irma shows up. She stops by Veronica's desk and I overhear her saying, "Well, you are getting bigger and bigger, huh? Not too attractive. Pregnant women look so . . . huge to me. Almost like barrels. I just don't know how they can stand it." Veronica's blushing hard. I think she's about to burst into tears.

I'm surprised to see Irma at the station. It hasn't even been a week since her husband was murdered. She's wearing jeans, much like everybody else. Except that jeans on Irma don't look the same as they do on anyone else. Her jeans hug her wonderful legs. They're so tight you can actually see the dimples on her knees. Her butt is very round and sexy. She has on a gold belt with some chains that clang with every step she takes. She's wearing a white silk blouse, opened to her cleavage; I don't think she's wearing a bra. At least I can't see a bra line under her blouse. Her breasts bounce a little, but they look very firm. Everybody stares at her. She's a knockout. A sexy knockout. And she knows it.

She walks over quickly to me as I'm about to open the door to the studio. "Do a good job," she says, "I'll be expecting your call for the contest at five-fifteen sharp. Don't be late."

"Yes, Ma'am," I answer. She looks very different to me now. Gone is the pout, the little girl demeanor, the giggle. She's in command, in charge. But the iciness of her stare has not changed at all.

From the studio, while a CD by Celine Dionne is playing, I call Lucia. She answers quickly. "Halifax residence."

"Lucia, it's Gloria from the radio station."

"Yes, Missy. You read book?"

"I read it. You were right. It might help Manny. Are you going to be there alone tonight?"

"Yes, Missy. The Mrs. go to big party at the museum. And Mr. Walter go out of town on business." *How strange. Now that they're alone in the big house, he leaves her to go out of town.*

"Can I come back later this evening," I ask, "to return the diary?"

"Yes, Missy. I be here all night."

"Alone?" I don't want anyone seeing me at the estate.

"Alone."

I hang up the phone and put on a Red Cross public service announcement. They're requesting blood donations. The supply has been getting dangerously low. My radio station has sponsored various radiothons where people donate blood and money. We, the staff of the station, show up at the "donation bank," entertain the donors, bring them donuts and coffee and interview some of them live on the air. Mr. Halifax was very conscious of our public service responsibility. He encouraged the entire staff to work for our city, to donate our time and efforts as often as possible. We never resented it. Most of us didn't. Almost all of us showed up at all the community events sponsored by the station. And Drew Kravitz, the program director, is very much involved in the spirit of community service. Unfortunately, the first day he attended the blood donation remote, he fainted at the sight of the first drop of blood! Nobody at the station lets him forget it.

While the public announcement is being aired, my studio phone rings. I answer it quickly, afraid that Lucia may have changed her mind about tonight. I feel extremely uncomfortable about having the diary in my possession. "Studio A, Gloria here."

"Hi, sweetcakes." The crazy fan. *Not again.*

"Good afternoon, sir, can I be of any help?" *That's a really smart question to ask.*

"You bet your sweet ass you can, sweetcakes."

"Yes, sir. What can I do for you? I need to be back on the air in thirty seconds." I'm not lying.

"Don't you dare hang up on me, you hear me? If you hang up or put me on hold, I'm warning you, you'll be very, very sorry."

I have to do something about this. The man is threatening me. "Sir, if you don't quit this," I feel myself growing bolder, "I'm going to turn on the mike so the whole world can hear what you're saying to me. Let me give you some friendly advice. Quit pestering me because I only need to press a small switch to let the whole world hear you." I hang up loudly. Maybe that will stop him.

The contest today is not too successful. We have no winners. Irma does a good job as Detective Sabrina, though. She's calm and cool as always and doesn't get distracted. She's a most surprising woman. All in all my shift is pretty good. I'm in a hurry. I'm not hanging around the studio after my shift is over. I'm raring to go. I want to see Peter and I want to get back to the Halifax house. At six o'clock sharp I sign off to my audience, pat Mr. Jenkins on the arm goodbye and dash to my car.

There's an outstanding invitation to Peter to have dinner with me tonight and I don't have anything ready. This will be the first time he's going to taste my cooking and I have nothing planned. I don't even know what time he's due over. *Oh my God, I hope he's coming over and that he didn't forget about our dinner together.* I'm worried that Lucia is waiting for me. I have to arrive at the estate before Irma shows up. And I'd like Peter there with me.

I call him as soon as I walk into my apartment.

"Peter Wilson, hello."–*Thank you God, I'll be good for a whole year.*

"Hi, Peter, Gloria."

"Well hello, kiddo, what's up?" *Oh no, he forgot about our dinner* "Don't tell me dinner's ready."

I smile, I giggle, I sigh. "Not yet, Peter. I . . . I . . . Wanted to ask you, well, would you like to go with me to deliver the diary to the maid? She's waiting for me and she'll be alone in the house for a while. I don't want Irma to find out that it disappeared and harm Lucia in any way."

"Sure. I'll pick you right up."

"Great. I'll wait for you at the entrance so you don't have to park."

"Ten minutes?"

"Ten minutes." *Bye, my love. My sweet. I'm going to be seeing you very soon.*

I change my jeans to a skirt. I want him to see my legs.

Dancer's legs. A little thin but firm. No stockings. I'm sure I'll be cold, but it's worth it. I take off my T- shirt and put on a light blue angora sweater. It's tight and it makes me look rounder, fuller. I bounce a little when I walk wearing my blue angora sweater. A little cologne behind my ears. I grab the diary and rush down the stairs.

The street is quite deserted and it's dark outside. At the corner of my block there's a fancy cigar shop that stays open late. A dark figure comes out of the store and starts walking toward me, slowly at first then a little faster. I can't distinguish his features, but his stance, his stature look familiar. He's approaching quite fast now and I have no doubt he's coming directly at me. A car is coming from the opposite direction and illuminates the man's face. He ducks into the first door- way. I could see his face only for a moment. But I know that face. I've seen it before. It's not the face of a friend.

Peter is here. He drives a black Porsche. I didn't expect to see him in a black Porsche. Nice, very nice. He opens the door for me and I climb in smiling at him and slide into the buck- et seat. Not very gracefully. He pats my hand lightly and by way of hello he says, "Lead the way." Oh boy. A drive to Potomac in rush hour. I'm starting to fret about the long drive. *Am I crazy? What do I care how long it's going to take? I'm sitting with Peter at my side. Very close to me. No distractions. No telephones, except for my cellular which I don't expect to use. No other people but him and me. God, Peter, you look so good. That denim jacket gives you such a devil-may-care look. And those jeans! Ah. Those jeans fit so snugly over your thigh, I'm dying to slide my hand up and down that thigh.* If I only dared.

So we travel for an hour or so. He has the radio on. Softly. I can barely hear the sounds of Schubert's Unfinished Symphony over the rumble of the engine. The car smells of leather and Peter's cologne. My legs feel cold. I'm wondering if Peter has noticed them. And whether I should tell him about the disturbing figure I just saw. *Could it be the caller?* I decide to keep it to myself.

Peter is very thoughtful. Very quiet. Both his hands are holding onto the wheel while I'm chattering away about life in a radio station. Once in a while I hear "Nice," or "Really?" or "Yes, yes, I'm listening."

"Tell me about you," I say. "About your life. I don't know much about you."

"Hmm," he says softly "there's not much to tell. My life hasn't been earth-shaking." *Oh, the quiet, unassuming type.*

"Are you an only child?"

"No, I have a younger brother. He's a professor of History at Penn State."

"Quite an accomplished family."

"My mother pushed us. Sweet, wonderful woman she was. She died of leukemia when I was in college. Destroyed us all. My father was never the same after that. He adored her. We all did."

"Do you have any kids?"

"No. We never did. My brother has two, though. Good kids, a boy and a girl. Both in college now. I guess it's costing him a fortune. And neither wanted to go to Penn State. Too close to their parents, they said. So they both are at Berkeley. My own alma mater."

"You're kidding me! You, staid, serious Peter a Berkeley graduate?"

"Sure thing. I graduated from its law school, too. Involved in all the demonstrations at that time, the love-ins, the craziness. Berkeley has changed a lot now. Much more conservative. I'm sure the fun has been plucked away. It's just another good school now. No more ferment. No more agitation. Too bad. It was great fun. Met my wife there. Beautiful woman. Petite, like you. We demonstrated together."

"Against what?"

"Against everything." We both laugh.

"Peter, what are your dreams? What do you want?"

"You mean besides being an incredibly good law professor?" He hesitates for a few seconds. "Well, if you really must know, my dream is to become a judge someday."

"A judge?"

"Yes, siree. I clerked for a judge in the D.C. Court of Appeals after graduating from law school. Loved it. Loved the research, the in-depth discussions, the intellectual approach to the law. So, that's what looks good to me. So far, though, I haven't been on the correct side of the political spectrum even to be eligible. Maybe someday. Maybe. . ."

"Peter?"

"Yes, babe. . ."

I reach for his hand. He grabs mine and intertwines our fingers. His hand is cool, smooth. I never realized how electric, how disquieting, how erotic the touch of a hand can be.

"Do you think that we. . . that us. . . that there's a chance. . . "

He interrupts me quickly and turns to me. I can just see

his wonderful liquid eyes. "You're my student, my dear. You're my student right now. I don't think it's a good idea. You know that I . . . I care . . ." He can't finish his sentence. I press his hand to my lips and whisper, "I understand."

"We must find a way to get to the ledger Irma mentioned in her diary," he says, all business.

"The payments to Verona?"

"Yes. I think it's important that we examine all angles. If Verona was indeed blackmailing Mr. Halifax, it's imperative we find out why. We need to talk to people who might have some information. We have to dig. Dig deep. Get all the facts. Maybe Irma and Walter had nothing to do with Halifax's murder and Verona did it. And didn't you tell me that he's still living at the Halifax estate?" I nod. "Well then, Irma, Walter and Lucia may be in danger."

"Do you think we should get to the ledger? That might tell us a lot. Irma indicated it was in a glass sculpture in the den."

"Well," Peter says. "Maybe you can convince the maid to let us into the house and we'll look for it in the den."

"I'm pretty sure Lucia doesn't want me inside the house. I think she's too scared to let us in. The last time she greeted me at the door and handed me the diary while we were both standing outside."

"You have to convince her to let us in. Tell her it might help Manny." He squeezes my hand.

We arrive at the estate. It looks as dark and forbidding as it did yesterday, but there's a full moon tonight and the rays are filtering through the trees and the windows, making the whole house shimmer.

"Some house," Peter says.

"Wait till you see their art collection. It is breathtaking." We're walking up the steps to the stained-glass doors. Lucia is by the door before I even have a chance to ring the bell.

"Good evening, Missy. Who is this?" She eyes Peter very suspiciously.

"This is Peter, Lucia. He's a lawyer who's helping Manny," I explain. "Peter, this is Lucia."

Peter smiles warmly, extending his hand and shaking Lucia's several times. Lucia doesn't return the warmth.

"Where's the book, Missy? I have to put it back."

"Here it is. It's going to be very helpful to Manny, I'm sure." I hand her the diary. She takes it brusquely and covers it immediately with her dark shawl. She turns to go back inside.

I run after her and hold her by her arm. "Lucia, excuse me, would it be possible for me to show Peter the house?" She pulls her arm from me.

"No, Missy. Is not possible. The Mrs. may come back soon. I don't have no permission to let somebody in the house." Her expression is grave. She seems quite upset at my suggestion.

"Lucia, it's very important we come in. Mr. Peter needs to look at the den where Mr. Halifax was murdered."

"It's critical to the case," Peter adds.

Lucia doesn't even look at him. "No, Missy. You ask the Mrs. If she say yes, then you come in. If she come now and she find you indoor, she be very mad at me. I not know what she do."

"I understand, Lucia. I assure you it'll only take five or ten minutes. No more. I promise." I'm pleading.

"No." She turns around to go into the house. Suddenly I utter a bone-chilling scream. It even scares me. Peter jumps and Lucia turns around quickly to look at me.

Peter walks over to me and puts an arm around my shoulders. "Gloria, what is it?" He's truly concerned.

"Missy, you O.K.?"

"Peter, I just saw a man behind the bushes. It's got to be that creep who's been calling me every day. I thought I saw him right outside my apartment tonight while I was waiting for you to pick me up. My God. He followed us here."

"Where is he?"

"I saw him go around the house. He must be hiding at the back of the house. We have to find him. We can't leave Lucia alone here. She could be in danger." They both look at me in astonishment.

"Lucia, quickly." I'm holding her by the arm again. "Do you have a flashlight? We should go together and maybe that'll scare him."

"I go call police," she says.

"That's fine," I say. "But if we wait too long he might escape. Let's go to the back of the house and try to find him—or at least scare him off."

"Gloria." Peter stops me in mid-stride. "Do you think that's smart? Shouldn't we all just wait for the police?"

"Sure we should," I say "But we really ought to see who's there. Confront him. Right now. Show him we're not afraid of him. Right now, before he can surprise us. Lucia, if you want us to wait here for you, we'll stay while you go find the flashlight."

"No, Missy. Is O.K. You can come in with me."

We walk into the enormous entrance hall. It's dark inside and very quiet. The only noise is the clacking of our shoes on the marble floor and the sounds of a TV very far away.

"Is anybody here, Lucia?" I ask in a whisper.

"No, Missy. That's TV in my room. The flashlights are here in the kitchen." She hands me two and I give one to Peter.

"Come with me, the two of you," I tell them. They follow me out of the house. Each one of us is carrying a flashlight.

We walk around the house into a garden barely visible in the moonlight. I walk a few paces behind them, and when they turn the corner, I make a mad dash back to the house. The door is unlocked. God, I hope I remember where the den is. It's so dark in here. I follow the hallway straight ahead, make a left. The mahogany doors. The den. Yes, I'm there. I push open the doors. My heart is beating so fast and hard I can actually hear it. I am dizzy with fright and with the thought that a dead body was lying on this floor. I turn on the flashlight. The blue oriental rug is no longer here. The floor is bare. The room feels so cold I can't even feel my hands. I almost drop the flashlight.

I'm hunting for the Therman Statom's glass sculpture. *Please let me remember what a Statom looks like.* I know I've seen his work at the Renwick Gallery. I remember it's made of small pieces of glass glued to larger painted panels. Above the chimney, on the mantle, I see a little glass house, maybe twelve by twelve inches that looks familiar. I move a chair over, climb on it and stick my hand inside the open front entrance of the house. I take out a small piece of lined paper that was leaning on the inside of the front wall of the glass house. I scratch my hand against the glass sides of the door. The paper is fancy. It feels almost like silk.

14

"You're a very clever girl." Peter is helping me prepare dinner. We stopped by the Natural Market and stocked up on chicken, rice, and clams. Peter bought me a bunch of gardenias. He remembered I once mentioned that those are my favorite flowers. Their aroma is magnificent. The whole apartment smells of gardenias. I place them in a small glass vase on the counter, close to where we're cooking and I bend down every so often to inhale. Peter looks at my angora sweater every time I bend down. I clean the scratch on my hand. He takes it and dabs gently at it with a towel.

I'm preparing a *paella* for Peter and me. It's going to take a long time to get ready, but we're not in a hurry. He opens a bottle of Spanish red wine and we have a few sips of the wine with the Spanish olives we just bought. A CD of Chopin's Nocturnes is playing. Such romantic, lyrical music. Its uninhibited emotional longing reflects my feelings for Peter. It's a magnificent evening.

I'm cleaning the clams, to put them in the rice that has taken a rich amber color with the saffron. I've just put a flan in the oven; it should be ready for desert. I hope Peter is impressed. I turn around from the sink where I'm standing to look at him. He's leaning against the counter just a few paces away from me. The kitchen is so small I only need to reach out to touch him. He's looking at me and smiling. The kitchen is hot and his face is flushed, making his eyes look almost violet. He's holding the glass of wine in one hand and the other hand is stuck in his jeans pocket. His shirt sleeves are rolled up and I can see his muscular forearms. Tanned. No wedding band. Just a black leather strap with a square watch. Masculine. I smile back at him and wipe my forehead with my arm.

"Yes, you're a clever girl. How did you come up with the idea of the stalker?"

"Oh," I answer as nonchallantly as I can. "It just sprang into my head at that moment. Some crazy person has been calling me at the station a lot and I thought I might have seen him this evening, while I was waiting for you. So I came up with the idea to distract Lucia."

"Brilliant. Although I don't like to hear that someone's been bothering you."

"Don't worry about it. I'm being very careful." I like his concern.

"The *paella* is starting to smell very good," he says. "I'm starving."

"It needs another thirty minutes. Come, let's sit in the living room and we'll discuss our next move."

On the living room table lies the piece of paper I stole from Mr. Halifax's den. It's a linen bond memo; its written lines are very close together–in small graceful letters in black ink. It has an entry date–the first day of the month–for every month of the last two years. There's an entry of an amount of money for each date, and the letters R.V. at the end of the entry. For some months the figure is larger than for others, especially toward the end of the year, but it never falls below $5,000 a month. And there is not one single month missing in the ledger.

We haven't discussed the ledger sheet. For some reason we tacitly agreed not to talk about the Halifax affair while we were coming home.

Now Peter says, "It's strange that Halifax would be making such large payments to his chauffeur."

"Sure is," I agree. "At least sixty-thousand a year." And why would Halifax himself be making the payments? It's well known at the station that all Halifax employees, including his personal employees like Lucia and the gardeners, get paid by the same accounting firm, Cole & Cole, that pays our checks at the station. We found out about it when there was a mix-up and all the checks that were supposed to go to his house came to the station with ours. We had to send our receptionist to deliver the checks to Mr. Halifax's house that same afternoon. I helped answer the phones while she drove to Potomac. No one thought it was funny that his pool man was making more money than some of us."

143

"Well, then, if Verona was getting paid by the accounting firm, why was Halifax keeping the ledger on him? And if he wasn't being paid by the accountants, why not?"

"I know a way to find out if the accountants have Verona on the payroll. I can ask Natalie, our business manager. She knows everything that goes on in Payroll. I've got to convince her, however, to tell me. She's very protective about Mr. Halifax's financial affairs."

"Do that tomorrow, if you can."

"It'll have to wait until Monday."

"Monday then," he says. "Meanwhile, we have all weekend to figure out how to flush out Verona."

All weekend, he said. All weekend. Is he expecting to spend both Saturday and Sunday with me? Please God. I don't know what I've done to deserve this but thank you, thank you.

Dinner is very good indeed. Much better than I expected. I really wanted to show off to Peter. I think I succeeded. The gardenias exude such a sweet, wonderful scent, the paella is close to perfect, and the flan, though still a little warm, is creamy and not too sweet. The sugar melted to perfection. Mouth-watering.

Peter finishes everything on his plate and asks for seconds. "You're a wonderful cook, you know? Where did you learn to cook like this?"

"My mother."

"Do you cook like this every night? Who do you cook for usually?"

Is he trying to find out if I have a boyfriend? A lover?

"No, I don't cook like this every night. Just for special occasions, when I have friends over." I don't want to reveal to him much, even though my scorecard consists of only two serious affairs over the years, neither of which amounted to much. One was in college, with a physics graduate student, and one was in New Bern, with the news director of a local TV station. Both fizzled out after a couple of months. There wasn't much passion on my side, and I'm looking for a passionate, crazy, all-consuming love affair. I'm not about to tell Peter any of that.

"You do that often?" he asks, reaching for my hand.

I squeeze his hand and feel my face burning with pure pleasure. "Whenever I have a chance."

"Well, I'd like to come here often, if you'll invite me. But only if you'll allow me to help with the cooking. I'm not bad in the kitchen, you know. Living alone for five years, well, I had to learn a thing or two in order to survive." He's saying this matter-of-factly but I glean traces of pain, of longing, of loneliness.

"I understand." I don't want to hear about his past life, about his loves and his pains. Not now. Not yet.

We're sitting around my little dining table—over strong, steaming espresso, in flickering candlelight. I brush aside a few breadcrumbs absentmindedly. Peter has put on a Bach clavier concerto. The gardenias perfume the air. Peter starts caressing my hand. He gently kisses the scratch, which is very faint by now.

"How can we get Verona to talk to us?" he asks me, and I snap back to reality.

"I'll have to think about it. Maybe I can come up with a contest where he's forced to call me or I can call him. I'll give it some thought."

"Does your supervisor give you freedom to conduct your show as you see fit?" He's stirring his espresso very slowly. His eyes look sleepy. He's starting to look very, very tired.

"Not usually. We have a pretty tight format. He doesn't allow us to break the musical and programming format easily, unless we have a very good reason to do so. Manny and the morning team have more freedom. They also have a lot more experience and the program director pretty much lets them do as they see fit, as long as it is not too outrageous."

"Will he let you in this case?"

"If I come up with an interesting concept, I think he will."

"Let me help you clear the dishes, Gloria." He stands up abruptly.

I stand too. "No, thank you, Peter. Please don't work. You can help me next time." *When is next time? Should I invite him again? Now?* "When do you think. . . ?" I'm starting to become pushy with him and I don't like that at all. I'd like things to flow more naturally between us.

"I'm busy tomorrow," he says. "I'm judging a moot court competition for my regular law students. You're welcome to come and see it, if you'd like. It's at five at the law school." *Just like that. He's busy. His "regular law students." Ah, well. It's been a long lovely evening.*

"I'll see if I can make it." I blow out the last of the flickering candles. He caresses my hair as I bend down.

"I love the color of your hair. It looks like burnt cinnamon." *How can I not love this wonderful man?* He walks toward the closet to get his jacket. I'm walking right behind him. He stands by the door without opening it and I stand immediately behind him. Very close to him, expectantly, holding my breath. He turns abruptly, faces me, clasps my face with both his hands and gently, presses his lips to mine.

"Good night, kiddo. Oh, and by the way, you have very pretty legs." He walks out.

Good night, sweet Peter. Good night, my love.

I don't see Peter Saturday. I don't want to see his "regular law students" perform. I couldn't possibly compete with them.

He doesn't call all day Sunday. I spend the whole day devising new contests and sulking a bit. And catching up on my studies. At eleven o'clock I go to bed. It seems that the moment I turn off the light, the phone rings.

"Gloria, I'm sorry, sweetie. It's Peter. Did I wake you?"

"No, no Peter. I was just . . . studying," I lie.

"I'm sorry I didn't call you all weekend. I had to get out of town after moot court on Saturday. I just got back." No other explanation. And I cannot ask for more.

"No need to apologize," I say. But I sound self-conscious. Smug.

"Any developments with our ideas of flushing out Verona?"

"I've been working on some. Nothing definite yet." *He's not asking me about my weekend. Has he spent the weekend with someone else? He must have.* My apartment feels very cold. I shiver under the blanket and pull it tighter around me. The bed feels empty. I cuddle the phone next to my ear to feel closer to him.

"Peter. . ."

"Yes, babe?"

"I. . . I'll see you in class tomorrow."

"I certainly hope so. Let's get together for dinner afterward. I want to give you some details I learned from Manny's attorney."

"I'm looking forward to it."

"So am I, kid. You go to sleep now. Sleep tight."

"You too." *Why aren't you here? With me? Holding me in your arms.* I hang up the phone. Another sleepless, lonely night.

First thing Monday morning, I call Natalie, the business manager, to invite her to have lunch with me. She seemed very touched and eager. I make a reservation at Chez Michel, a fancy French restaurant close to the station. I need Natalie in an expansive and relaxed mood. I arrive quite early at the station. I'm wearing my blue business suit, high heels, and a silk white shirt. My power uniform. I think it's the first time I've dressed like this to come to the station and people stare at me. Drew Kravitz smiles at me when he sees me come in. "What's the occasion, Gloria? Interviewing for a better job? How come you're here so early?" He pushes his glasses up his long nose. They are always sliding down. "I wish all my deejays dressed like that to work. It would give some class to the station."

"Thank you, Drew. No, I'm not looking for another job.

My job's good here." Drew smiles broadly. I like the man. He's always polite, friendly. He treats his subordinates, all the deejays, fairly. I have played some tricks on him sometimes and the poor man has absolutely no sense of humor. But he has never rebuked me for making him the butt of some of my jokes.

I walk past Irma's office. The door's open and the office is empty. I cross the hall, past three other offices, to Natalie's sanctuary. We call it the heart of the station, because all the juices of the station flow from there. We all have to go there every other Friday to collect our checks. Mine is pretty small. They take so many deductions that I can barely afford to live in D.C. No complaints, though, I love my job.

Natalie is sitting at her desk. There are no windows in her office. She likes it, she says, because she wants no distractions. The desk is oversized and is always stacked with papers. In one corner of the room there's an enormous safe and next to the safe there's a heater. Natalie is always cold. She wears a sweater even in the middle of summer. "Do they have to keep the air conditioning so cold?" is her constant complaint during the warm months, when everybody else seems to be melting. She looks up as I walk into her office. She has brown curly hair, tinged with gray here and there and a long bony face, with no makeup except for a mauve-colored lipstick.

"Ready to go?" I ask. "Reservations are for twelve noon." I start to perspire the moment I set foot in her office. Drew says you can grow orchids in here.

"Just give me a moment, will you, Gloria? I have an emergency brewing here." Natalie always has an emergency brew-

149

ing. She's always in a rush and she's always taking work home. There have been so many times, I can't even remember how many, when I've seen her hurry by, on her way out, laden down with file folders, ledgers, sheaf of papers. She's a widow, has no children, and the station seems to be her entire life. It's her lifeline to sanity. "Without this work I would go stir crazy," she always says. She knows everything that goes on at the station, and when we need information about anything or anybody, we go straight to her. Sometimes she gives us the information, sometimes she doesn't, depending on her mood. She appears to be lonely, however. She doesn't seem to have any friends. No one invites her out. I'm not sure why. Not to lunch, not to have drinks when the rest of the gang gets together. Once in a while, I take her out to a fast food place downstairs. She gulps down her food and zips back to her desk in fifteen minutes. So today I'm taking her to Chez Michel for a long, relaxed lunch. My treat.

We walk out together into the street. Chez Michel is just down the block on Wisconsin Avenue. Very elegant, starched white table cloths, fresh flowers on every table, fine crystal and fine china. The entire place shimmers. It's also very expensive. I'll have to be careful with my expenditures the entire month. I've been here only once before, when my parents took me out to lunch with them the day before they moved to Florida. It was a bittersweet lunch goodbye. They were excited about their new adventure, but sad to leave their little girl behind. My father's eyes were glistening the entire lunch. He said it was an allergy to something. He has no allergies.

Natalie, dressed all in gray–heavy gray sweater, gray pants, gray wool socks and a knitted gray scarf–walks a little stooped. I don't think she's old. She just looks old. It's very windy and cold outside. The leaves are whipping around at our feet. Natalie's scarf hits me on the face once or twice. She walks down the street in front of me at a very brisk pace. It's surprising. I'm half running to catch up to her.

We sit down at a corner table, near the window, where we can see people walk by. It's lunch hour and the streets are very crowded.

"Mesdames, anything to drink?"

Natalie orders hot strong coffee and a kahlua, I ask for a glass of the house white wine, to keep her company. One's my limit, though, because I have to go on the air and wine makes me sleepy. I order a shrimp salad. She orders onion soup, a T-Bone steak, well done, with french fries, and a side order of house salad with Roquefort dressing. Double serving of dressing, please. Where does she put all that food? She's nothing but skin and bones.

We talk about the station. We discuss Mr. Halifax and Manny and the future of each one of the members of the station's staff. After she's had two or three kahluas I broach the subject.

"Listen, Natalie, do you know if all of Mr. Halifax's employees, even the ones at home, are paid by Cole & Cole?"

"Yes, we all are. All of us." She's talking much slower now. "We all get paid by Cole & Cole. Every single one of us."

"Even the maid and the chauffeur?"

"Yes."

"Do they make a lot of money?" I'm not sure I'm going to get an answer to this.

"More than you, yes."

"A lot more?"

"Well, the maid makes more than twenty-eight." I figure that's over five hundred dollars a week. *Yep. She sure gets paid more than I.*

"And the chauffeur?"

"He also makes more than you."

"How much more?"

"Well, I'm not at liberty to reveal that sort of information, just let me say it's between thirty thousand and thirty-five thousand." *Wow! Plus the sixty grand he's making on the side. Not a bad deal being Mr. Halifax's driver. Not a bad deal at all.*

"Why are you asking me all these questions?" Natalie suddenly demands.

"Just curious. Have you been to Walter's gallery yet?"

"Haven't been invited yet." She sulks a little. Takes a sip of her Kahlua.

"Would you like another drink?'

"That would be very nice." A smile. A glint in the eye. Not much work will be done by Natalie this afternoon, I'm afraid.

"Is he doing all right at the gallery?" I ask.

"Well, if you consider losing ten to fifteen thou' a month doing all right then I guess you can say he's doing all right." That's the way Natalie talks. Never a completely straight answer. "Cole & Cole was sending him checks to cover his losses every month. He asked me just last month if we could conceal this from his father. I told him no. Just plain no. He got mad at me, but I don't care. I don't like him much. He's so loud and he's such a lousy businessman. And he was always looking for a way to get more money from his father. No siree, I don't like him much at all."

Good old Natalie. She has eaten only half of her food and asks to take the rest in a doggy bag.

"I'll wrap it up for you, madam," the waiter says. "We don't have doggy bags at Chez Michel."

Back at the station Veronica hands me a phone message. It's from Manny. He's out on bail.

15

Brilliant ideas seem to come from nowhere. Right now, while I have a Billy Joel CD on the air, I've come up with a contest that I think will draw Verona out. I need to get Drew's approval immediately. I've got to talk him into it. But Drew doesn't like to make fast decisions. "Let me sleep on it" is his standard response to almost any request. He must answer me today, though.

During the four o'clock news segment I run into his small office, next to the studio. It's cramped with CD's from floor to ceiling. A few old LP's are lying on the floor and there's a poster of Mariah Carey right above his desk. Drew is bent over his desk looking at a play list. His nose looks enormous when he's gazing down and his glasses are halfway down his nose. The glasses are so large that they seem to cover his entire face. His hand is resting on a framed picture of his pretty wife and three small boys.

I walk in breathlessly. "Drew. . ." He doesn't like it when we leave the studio in the middle of our shifts. Unless, of course, it's some sort of emergency. "You have to approve my new contest. I want to start it this afternoon."

"What contest? What's the rush?" He adjusts his tortoise-shell glasses. His Adam's apple bobs up and down when he talks. I always stare at it and wonder if he can feel it as it moves.

"People have been complaining to me that they can't get through to me when my contest is on. They say that the phone lines are always busy."

"That's good, Gloria. That's not a bad thing. That means that a lot of people are calling you. Your contest is getting popular."

I know that. I go on with my pitch without listening to him. "Drew, I want to have a call-out once in a while–just a person at random." Of course I'm lying. I know exactly the person I'm going to call. "I'll ask them questions on the air, so everyone can play along, and if the persons I call answer the questions correctly I'll give them a big prize. Five thousand dollars. With your permission, of course. It'll really spice up the contest. It'll bring us more listeners. You know it will." I know this will get him.

"What kind of questions?" *Ah! I've got him.*

"Just questions relating to my contest," I say as casually as possible.

"Let me see your questions and I'll sleep on it. If I like them you can start your new contest next week."

It has to be today. I have to get his permission now. I just keep at him. "I really would like to start this afternoon," I insist. "It's quite important." *Bold move.* "The ratings period is almost over." *Clever move.*

"Are they hard questions?"

"No, quite easy, really. People will enjoy them and I think they'll play along."

"OK, then. As long as your calls are made at random."

"Oh, they will be. Thank's, Drew." *My God, I didn't know I could lie so easily.*

I sprint back to the studio. Tim Elias is almost finished with the news when I walk in. He gives me a panicked look as if afraid I wasn't coming back.

"Here I am." I put on the earphones, smile at him as sweetly as I can, and speak brightly into the microphone:

"Welcome back, folks. Gloria Berk here at WVVV with two more hours of sweet music and exciting detective work. Let's listen to a wonderful rendition of 'Strangers in the Night' by who else but Ol' Blue Eyes himself." The lunch wine is affecting my brain, I'm sure.

I look for the Halifax home phone number and dial. Irma is not at the station yet. I'm hoping she won't pick up the phone.

"Hello, Halifax residence." *Good, it's Lucia.*

"Lucia, hi. Gloria here."

"Good afternoon, missy. How are you?"

"Fine, Lucia. Listen. It's very important for me to talk to Robert Verona later on. Will he be home?"

"Missy, I not know. Sometimes he drive Mr. Walter or the

Mrs. He usually come home at five if he not drive no one."

"Lucia, please keep him there if you see him. Tell him it's important. Tell him he could make a lot of money. I'm going to be calling him a few minutes after five . . . And now folks, Natalie Cole with 'Unforgettable'." I put on another CD and hope Drew isn't listening to my show today. It's really quite bad, totally disorganized. "Can you make sure, Lucia, that he's there when I call? Please, it's very important."

"I try, Missy Gloria. I no promise nothing."

"Thank you, Lucia." The CD is over, I have to stay focused. "You're listening to WVVV, Gloria Berk here, we're in our ten-in-a-row segment. Following this, let's all thrill to the warm voice of Barbra Streisand singing 'People'."

I've got to hurry and finish putting together the new contest. I only have one chance to flush out Verona. I mustn't fail. Sue walks into the studio looking quite happy. Her smile is broad, showing off her pretty teeth.

"Hi, girlie," she says. "Everything going O.K.?"

"Yes, Sue, no problem here. What can I do for you?" She never walks into the studio when I'm in the middle of a shift unless I made a terrible mistake and she spotted it. It happened once in New Bern. I had forgotten where I was and gave out the wrong call letters. Very bad mistake. Never happened again.

"Oh, nothing much," she answers. "Can we have a drink together after you finish here? I'll wait for you. I had my date with Ron Douglas." She winks at me.

"And now, please stay tuned for the following commercial message. Don't go away. I have a surprise for you, devoted listeners, as soon as we come back. Stay tuned." And I let them hear about the newest book shop in town. "How was it?" I ask. "You had a good time?" I really cannot pay too much attention now. I have to work on my contest.

"I don't want to talk right now. Let's go out for a drink at six."

"I can't, Sue. I have a class tonight."

"Oh, that's right. You can't miss an evening of school to spend some time with your friend." She sounds angry and disappointed. She turns around very fast to leave the studio.

"How about tomorrow?" I call after her. "Breakfast, lunch or dinner. You name it." I really want to let her tell me about her new love interest. She's so excited.

"We'll see. I'm going now. See you tomorrow." She's mad. I know she's mad. I'll have to make it up to her.

My ten-in-a row segment is over and I go back on the air.

"I hope you enjoyed the romantic sounds of Mel Tormé. A great mellow voice, don't you agree? Now it's my pleasure to inform you we're starting a brand new contest immediately after the news. Don't go away. I'll be calling one lucky person in our listening area. If I call you and you can spell three words correctly, I'll give you five thousand dollars. As simple as that. So stay tuned. It could be you I'll be calling. And now, here's Tim Elias with the news. Good afternoon, Tim."

"Good afternoon, Gloria. It's five o'clock and now the news . . ."

At exactly ten after five I dial the Halifax number. I know it by heart now. My palms are sweaty. My heart is pounding.

I'm on the air and I can't make any mistakes.

"Hello?" It's Lucia.

"Good afternoon. This is Gloria Berk from WVVV, your love songs station. I'd like to speak to Mr. Robert, please. Is he there?" *Help me, God.*

A pause. And then, "Hello," a deep, curt voice answers.

"Mr. Robert?"

"Yes."

"Mr. Robert from Potomac? I won't reveal your last name on the air." *I don't want anybody at the station to recognize who I have on the line. Family members and employees of the owner are barred from participating in our contests.*

"Yes. My name is Robert and I live in Potomac." There is impatience in his voice.

"Mr. Robert, you're on the air. This is Gloria Berk, from WVVV. You're the lucky contestant of the day. I'm going to give you three words related to my 'Crime in the Afternoon' contest. If you spell the three correctly I'll give you five thousand dollars. But you must spell the three words correctly. Do you understand?"

"Yes."

"First word: Intent." I can't make it too hard because he might make a mistake right away and I don't want to lose the connection. But it has to be hard enough to make the contest seem real. After a few seconds the sounds come out very, very slowly:

"I-N-T-E-N-T."

"Excellent, Mr. Robert. You've spelled it correctly. Second word: Post-Mortem." I know I'm taking a chance here. He could miss this one.

Again the letters come out very slowly:" P-O-S-T-M-O-R-T-E-M." It's clear that he's less sure this time.

"Very, very good. Two down and one more to go. And now for the third word for the grand prize of five thousand dollars, are you ready, Mr. Robert?"

"I'm ready."

"Please spell for us the word payoffs, as in blackmailer's payoffs," I add for effect.

Silence on the other end of the line. "Mr. Robert? No guess? Please stay on the line. I want to tell you if you won anything for the first two correct answers."

I quickly go to a commercial. Verona has not hung up.

"Robert, does the word blackmailer scare you? I have the ledger Mr. Halifax kept."

"Where? What?"

"Listen to me. I don't have too much time to talk to you. If you don't want me to call the police immediately, you will meet me and you'll tell me about the ledger."

"I don't know what the hell you're talking about, lady. You're crazy."

"Yes you do. . . And now ladies and gentlemen, here's another musical giant for your enjoyment." I put on a CD in the machine without even noticing whether it was on today's rotation. *My God, if Drew's listening, I'll be out of a job. No doubt.* "Listen, Robert, you'd better meet with me and talk to me. If you're in any kind of trouble I know lawyers who can help you. I expect to see you tomorrow evening at six-thirty at the Pines of Rome restaurant. You know where that is. And you'd better come alone." I hang up on him.

Not just gutsy, but also really stupid. And I've never had a worse show in my life. But I'm lucky, Sue's gone, and evidently Drew wasn't listening. Or maybe he's just given up on me.

Class with Peter is a breeze today. I studied all weekend and feel prepared and relaxed in class. I also look good, with my black pants and black turtleneck. I feel stunning. I sit in the first row and he calls on me two or three times. With easy questions. He allows me to show off a bit. I'm happy. I think he is too.

At the end of class I climb up the few steps to the podi um where he is, as usual, surrounded by students. I admire him as I wait. His soft gaze, his warm, friendly smile. I especially like the way he looks tonight with his gray shirt open at the collar, just a tuft of chest hair showing.

"Gloria." A strong arm hugs my shoulders. "Have a drink with me tonight," Steve whispers.

I turn my head and gently peel his arm off me. "I can't tonight. How about this weekend? Here's my phone number. Call me." I pull a piece of paper out of my notebook, quickly jot my number down and hand it to him. He looks at it, smiles and puts it in his shirt pocket. "You've got it."

I look up at Peter. He's staring at me and walking toward me, nodding and smiling.

"You studied hard, kiddo. You were prepared."

"Just a little." I can't contain my pride.

"You hungry?"

"Starving."

"Good. I picked out a nice quiet place for us to go." *Great! This was worth waiting for the whole weekend.* "By the way," he continues "there's someone I want you to meet." He looks up at the rows of seats and waves. "That's Jenna Rogers, Manny's attorney, and a good friend of mine." I follow his gaze to a woman in the last row waving back at him. I can't really distinguish her features. "She was kind enough to accept my invitation to join us for dinner." She stands up. My stomach hurts. I'm so disappointed.

She comes down the steps slowly. Brown eyes, brown glossy hair cut shoulder length. Very straight, very glossy. She's tall, slender. Nice-looking legs in tan stockings and navy blue pumps. Navy skirt covering her knees, striped white and blue shirt buttoned at the neck. Blue jacket tossed carelessly on her arm. I can't take my eyes off her the whole time she's walking down the steps.

Long fingers grab my hand strongly. She pumps my arm once or twice. "So, you're Gloria, Manny's friend. He says very nice things about you."

"Thank you."

Peter is smiling broadly. "Well," he says, "now that we are all acquainted, let's eat. Did you drive, Jenna?" *His manner is too friendly with her.*

"No, I took the Metro from my office downtown. You remember, I live just down the street on Mass Avenue."

"Fine. You ride down with me. You have a car, right, Gloria?"

"Yes," I mumble.

"O.K. Meet us at the Rathskeller down Wisconsin

Avenue. We'll just catch up on old times and won't discuss Manny's case until we all meet at the restaurant."

"Fine." I mumble again.

She's a pretty woman, Jenna Rogers. Even her name is pretty. I watch her smile at Peter and notice how lean and tough and soft and graceful she is, all at once. Beautiful eyes. Very soft brown. Beautiful skin. When I walked into the restaurant, they were already sitting at a table and had ordered red wine for all of us.

"Jenna was my star student some years ago," Peter tells me. "She went to work for the D.A.'s office. Three years ago she opened her own law firm." Peter is gloating.

"With three other women." She smiles at him.

"Sounds nice." *I have to control myself. After all, she's here to talk to me about Manny. Where are my priorities?*

We all order sauerbraten and potato dumplings. Peter pushes the red wine aside just after a few sips and asks for a beer. Jenna and I drink the red wine.

"Peter tells me you really believe Manny is innocent." She's smiling at me. Her tone is very friendly. *Too friendly.*

"I know he's innocent." I sound defensive. "He's a very good, honorable, decent man." *Couldn't I come up with more adjectives?*

Jenna stops smiling and looks at Peter and then at me. Her eyes have become hard. "Well, I'm afraid the D.A. has a very good case against him. The evidence is substantial."

"You mean the letter opener," I say with a dismissive wave of my hand.

"Yes, and the fingerprints both on the letter opener and a drinking glass. Also a neighbor of the Halifaxes is ready to testify that he saw Manny at the estate on the night of the murder."

I feel the food getting stuck in my throat. "That's not possible."

"Why not? Do you know where he was around six on the evening of Monday, October 6?" This is not a simple question. It's hard-hitting cross examination.

"I'm sure he was at the station. He's always there for his shift from six to midnight."

"It's no use lying," she says sharply. "Lying is not going to help Manny in any way. I have a log of that night. Radio stations do keep logs, don't they?"

My heart is sinking. She called me a liar in front of Peter. Worse yet, I was lying. "Yes, they do. We keep logs."

"Well, we know from those logs that it was you who was on the air at six o'clock that evening. Manny does not have an alibi until well after seven-thirty."

Oh, God. "What are we going to do to help him? We must do something. Anything." I'm angry and desperate, and that's the way I sound. I can't help it.

She softens a little. "I'm not sure yet. I just took the case on Friday. I was tied up in court on another case. So I've had very little time to look deeply into this matter. I just don't know yet what our options are, Gloria. I haven't been able to prepare." *Sure you've had little time to look into it. Especially if you spent the weekend with Peter.* "I got Manny out on bail," she continues. "It wasn't easy. He's a flight risk, you know. All his family lives in Los Angeles. Also, he hasn't been forthcoming with me about the affair."

"What affair?" I pounce on her.

Peter reaches for my hand and pats it. Jenna notices it.

"The affair with the fifteen-year-old girl," Jenna answers.

"He didn't have an affair with her," I shoot back.

"Gloria, listen to me." She's talking very softly. I'm having trouble hearing her even in this quiet restaurant. "I think he did. Mr. Halifax himself visited the girl and the mother, together with their attorney Sconix. He offered them money, cars, anything, if they would back off on their accusation. They wouldn't. The mother told him in detail how Manny had forced the girl to have oral sex with him. In the studio. And Mr. Halifax confronted Manny with this information the very day he was killed."

"How do you know this? I'm sure Manny didn't tell you any of this."

"No, he didn't. But Mr. Halifax and his attorney, Arnold Watson, talked to Manny. I think you've met Watson, haven't you?" I nod. "Well, Watson told me the whole story. And Watson emphasized that Manny didn't deny anything." I must have blanched because Peter is really squeezing my hand.

"I'm sorry, Gloria." Jenna says. " But I'll do whatever I can to help Manny."

Yeah, you do that. You do that, Jenna.

16

"I know where you live and I know what you do." *Oh no, it's the weirdo again. He's been calling more often now, and each call makes me more uneasy.*

"Sir, would you like me to broadcast your voice to the whole world? I'll just turn on the mike, you know? Do you understand me?" My voice is becoming shrill. I'm starting to sound desperate.

CLICK, he's gone. I don't know what to do. I probably should tell Sue about this guy. But she has enough problems at the station as it is. Maybe Peter. Maybe it's time to ask him for advice. God, I don't want to appear like I don't know how to take care of myself. I think I'll tell him anyway. It might bring us closer together. *I wish.*

When my shift is over, I ask Mr. Jenkins, once again, to

walk me to my car. I'm not exactly afraid. I'm uneasy. And the garage is deserted at this hour. . .

Mr. Jenkins, kind old soul, accompanies me and chats about the new contest. "I like it, Miss Gloria. I don't know why the contestant yesterday couldn't answer the third word. It wasn't very hard."

"Sometimes people get very nervous when they know they're on the air, Mr. Jenkins. And what seems easy to the rest of us seems very confusing to them."

"I guess so."

The garage is empty except for my car and one or two others.

"Here's my car, Mr. Jenkins. I don't know how to thank you."

"No problem, Miss. You have yourself a good night, you hear? And drive safely. I'll see you tomorrow."

"Thank's again. You have a nice evening, too, Mr. Jenkins."

I slide into the car and start the ignition. Mr. Jenkins waves goodbye and retreats. I wish he would stay just a little longer. But he's been away from his post too long. His limp becomes more obvious as he hurries away.

I drive up to the top of the ramp and toward the electric door. I insert my magnetic card and wait for the door to open. As soon as it starts to open, I accelerate and I'm halfway under it when my car comes to a complete stop. I'm petrified the door will slide down and come crashing onto my car. I keep pushing on the gas pedal but nothing happens. The car is dead. I turn off the engine and try to start it again. It's totally dead.

Suddenly I notice a man approaching. *Thank you God, I'm*

sure he'll be able to help me. I smile at him and open the window. "I don't know what happen . . ." *Oh my God. I recognize the face. I looks like the same man who approached me near my apartment. It's the man who was standing near my car outside the National Cathedral the day of the memorial service for Halifax. The fan who knows me. The one who knows my name. The one who couldn't get through the phones. Who is he? I know him. I've seen him somewhere else before those times. But where? When?*

"Hi, Gloria." The voice is deeper than I remembered. More menacing. The sleeves of his black T-shirt are rolled over his muscular arms, covered with copper-colored hair. His pale blue eyes are incisive, boring into mine. I want to look away, but I don't want him to think I'm afraid. I hold his cold stare.

"What . . . can you help me?" *I know him. I know him. God, who is this creep?*

"Why? You never want to talk to me. Why should I help you?"

"What are you doing here?"

"I told you. I know everything you do. Everywhere you go. I needed to see you. You hung up on me today again. You're a very bad girl. I'm going to have to teach you a lesson so that you start behaving better with me." He's smiling as he talks. I'm revolted by the sight of his dingy, dirty teeth. *I've seen those teeth before. Those nicotine-stained teeth. The chipped front tooth. Of course, of course. He's the waiter. Where? Where? The waiter of the Pines of Rome restaurant. Of course. Oh God, please. Let someone else pull out now. Maybe someone can help me. Stay calm. Stay calm.*

"Aren't you . . . ?

He keeps coming closer. "It doesn't matter any more who I am. Does it? You never really looked at me before. Did you?" His voice is rising. "How many times did I serve you? Left other people to rush to your side? Did you ever even notice me?"

He's very close to me now and I start to close the window, but he abruptly reaches in and grabs me by the hair. I scream as hard as I can.

"Open the door, Gloria." His voice is very quiet, barely a whisper. "Let me in. I won't hurt you. I only want to be with you. I want to talk to you. Open the door."

"Let go! Let go of me!" I scream at him. I try honking the horn but it doesn't work anymore with the engine off. I never got it fixed. *What an idiot.* And my cellular phone is in my bag, lying on the back seat of the car. *Absolutely brilliant.* Suddenly, an enormous figure comes out of nowhere, yanks his arm from inside my car, grabs him by the back of the shirt and pulls him away from me. *Oh God, thank you.* The huge man is pouncing on the stalker. Hitting him very hard in the face. Even with the window closed I can hear the blows. The big man throws my stalker to the ground and starts kicking his ribs and his head. Hard. Blood pours out of the stalker's mouth and nose. The stalker isn't moving at all. I'm riveted by the sight of him. I want to look away but I'm unable to.

The big man returns to my car. I can't believe it. It's Robert Verona looming, looking down at me. I don't know whether to thank him or run away.

"You all right?" Booming, powerful voice.

"Yes. Thank you. How lucky you were here. How come you're here?"

"Let's see what's wrong with your car." He pushes the car the rest of the way out the door and keeps pushing until we're in the alley just behind the building. The electric door comes down with a loud crash. He opens the hood of the car and bends down to look inside. I'm still sitting inside the car, debating whether I should go out and pretend I understand what he's doing with the engine or whether I should just drive away as soon as he's fixed it. We're in a very deserted alleyway. There's no one here. The only witnesses are trash cans scattered everywhere. Even with my window closed, I can smell the garbage littering the uneven pavement.

I grab my bag with my phone inside it, get out and go around to the front of the car next to Robert. The top of my head doesn't even reach his shoulder. I'm not carrying any weapons. My father once gave me a can of mace. "A girl needs protection," he said, just before he left for Florida. I promptly put it in a drawer in my bathroom and totally forgot about it. Until now.

"Look," Robert says. "Somebody loosened the ignition wire that runs from the starter coil to the distributor cap. Somebody tampered with your car to make it stall right away. Wanted it dead. If one of the contacts gets loose, the car stalls and dies." He's pulling wires and showing me. I feign interest. "When you started moving the car," he continues, "the vibrations disconnected this wire from the starter coil. I just have to push the wire into the starter coil and I'll have the car running for you in no time."

"Robert, I thank you very deeply. You have no idea how much I appreciate this. What do we do about that creep?"

"Leave him there. He'll be all right. I barely touched him."

I smile. "Tell me, how come you're here?"

"I came to confront you. Nobody knows about Mr. Halifax's ledger. I was waiting to talk to you when you left the station." He's tinkering with the car. "There you are, good as new. I followed you to the garage. I wanted to be alone with you. When I saw the man approaching you and you were smiling, I thought he was your friend. And then I saw you were in trouble."

"Thank you, Robert. What do you mean confront?"

"I want the ledger back. And I want it now." The friendly tone is gone.

"I don't have it with me."

"You know, it was really dumb what you did. Calling me from the radio station."

"We need to talk, Robert. Please meet me at the restaurant." I certainly don't want to be alone with him in the car. And the alley is not exactly the place to accuse him of blackmail, possibly murder. "Please, Robert. I'm sure we can settle this. If you meet me there, I promise you I'll call my boyfriend to bring the ledger. He has it." I lied.

"What boyfriend? The murderer?"

"Who are you talking about?"

"That deejay. The fox. Whatever his name is."

"Manny? You're talking about Manny?"

"Yeah. Him. I don't wanna see him."

"Manny is not my boyfriend. He's not the one who has

the ledger. Won't you meet me?" I'm pleading by now. "Please, Robert."

He hesitates for a few seconds, looks at me and then at his watch. He scratches his chin. "If I meet with you, will you give me the ledger?"

"Yes."

"OK. Half an hour." He glances at his watch, and walks away.

I'm seated at the same table where I saw Verona sitting with the beautiful woman. I'm looking at the door expectantly. Nobody knows I'm meeting with him. Not even Peter. I'm not even certain he's going to show up. Suddenly he appears at the door, dwarfing the impressive gold and glass entrance. I can look at him better now. He's at least six-five and must weight two hundred and fifty pounds. A very impressive man. His black tailored pants are smudged–from the fight, I suppose. He's wearing a white shirt, and it has a slight rip on the sleeve. His usual bow tie is missing. I can see some blood spots on his blue satin jacket draped carelessly over one shoulder. His dark hair is freshly combed.

He approaches my table and sits down without uttering a sound.

"Do you want something to drink?" I ask.

"A beer."

I order a beer for him and an iced tea for me. I've got to keep my head clear.

"Thank's again for what you did for me, Robert."

"Don't mention it. I would've done it for anybody. Now,

let's talk. Where did you find the ledger?"

"In Mr. Halifax's den."

"How did you know it existed? How do you know it refers to me?"

"Irma's diary mentioned it and it mentioned you by name."

"She knew about it, then. Goddamn dame. Never mentioned a word to me."

"She knew about it."

"That dame was driving Mr. Halifax mad, do you know that? Always bugging him. Always fighting with him. Always asking him for things. Never a moment's peace in that goddamn house."

Now is the time for the hard questions. He can't harm me here; there are too many witnesses.

"Were you blackmailing Mr Halifax, Robert?"

He doesn't answer. He just sips his beer.

"I think you were, and maybe he got tired of your extortion. Right?" I look at him. He's looking away. "Did he stop paying you and threaten to expose you? Call the police? Is that why you killed him?"

He looks up sharply. His black eyes become coals. His pock-marked face becomes vivid red and starts twitching. He slaps the table with such enormous force that the iced tea spills out of my glass.

Everyone sitting in the quiet restaurant turns to look at us. The waiter starts walking very fast toward us. I hold my hand up in a reassuring gesture. "It's all right," I mouth.

Robert lets out a shrill laugh. It doesn't seem to come

from that huge frame.

"Kill him? Kill Mr. Halifax? You must be crazy, lady. I didn't kill Mr. Halifax. He was my livelihood. My supporter. My friend. Crazy dame. I wasn't even in Washington when he died."

"I don't believe you."

"I don't give a shit whether you believe me or not, you dumb, stupid broad."

"You were supposed to pick up Sue Hamilton the day of the murder and you weren't there. Were you?"

"I told you. I wasn't in Washington." He picks up his beer glass and continues sipping it. He doesn't even look at me. He's sipping away and wiping the foam from his lips with his sleeve. I keep staring at him. I'm hoping that he'll open up, somehow. He isn't a bad-looking man. His glossy dark hair is falling a bit over his eyes. His eyebrows are very dark and very bushy, peeking from behind his long hair. His full mouth is quite sensual. Not a bad-looking man at all.

He suddenly lifts his eyes, looks straight at me, half smiles and says in a whisper, "What the hell. With the murder and all it's going to come out anyway. Jesus God. I'm breaking a promise. May God forgive me for what I'm about to do." He pauses for a second, then goes ahead. "Mr. Halifax has a son. A baby son."

"With Irma?" I'm incredulous.

"No. Not with Irma. With someone else. Someone who doesn't live here."

"Who. Where does she live?"

"A beautiful girl. Gorgeous. Her name is Lila Hamilton.

She lives in New York."

"Hamilton?" I'm surprised at the name.

"Yes. Lila Hamilton. She's Sue's younger sister."

"Sue? My Sue? The general manager?"

"That's right. Your Sue. He met her in New Bern, when she went to visit her sister there. Sue introduced them."

"Halifax . . ."

"Yes. Mr. Halifax had an affair with her that started a few years ago. I used to take him to the hotel where they met, where she was waiting for him. She became pregnant. It was I who took her to George Washington Hospital to give birth. She had a baby boy two years ago. Donny. Mr. Halifax was crazy about the baby. Loved him so much. The money you saw listed on that ledger sheet is what he gave me to take to her once a month. I insisted I sign for it. I insisted I put my initials on that sheet."

"Why didn't he just wire her the money? Or send it by mail?"

"Because he wanted me to check on them. To make sure they were doing all right. That's where I was the day Mr. Halifax was killed. Sometimes he would go to New York himself and I would drive him. I was the one who always gave the money to Lila, though. He thought it would embarrass her if he handed her the money himself. The day he died was not a scheduled trip. Lila called to say that Donny was ill. He was running a very high fever. She was extremely anxious. So Mr. Halifax wanted to go see the baby. I was supposed to drive him the night he was killed. He couldn't go because he suddenly took very ill. He told me he felt very dizzy and weak. So he asked me to go by myself. I did."

"Robert," I say in my sternest voice, "I've been told that Mr. Halifax couldn't have any children."

" Who told you that stupidity? Of course he could."

"Aren't Walter and Patrick adopted?"

"Yes, they are. He didn't want to have any children of his own. He had a genetic disease. He didn't want to pass it down."

"And Donny?"

"Donny is his. His own flesh and blood. He was not a planned baby. At the beginning, Mr. Halifax didn't want to accept it. He wanted Lila to abort the baby. But Lila's a Catholic and wouldn't have an abortion. I heard them once in the car arguing about it. She left Washington and went to New York to live with her mother after she had the baby. You've seen her," he suddenly adds.

"Who?"

"Lila. You've seen Lila. She's the woman who was sitting here the evening you came in. I was afraid you would tell Mrs. Halifax about it."

"That beautiful black-haired woman?"

"That's Lila." I thought I heard so much wistfulness, so much longing in those words. "I called her to tell her about the murder and she insisted on coming down here for the memorial service. Her sister Sue doesn't speak to her. We didn't want the Halifax family to see her sitting alone. That's why I was with her during the service. She's devastated. She truly loved that man. And I don't know what she is going to do now without him. How she will be able to afford to raise

Donny. I hope Mr. Halifax has provided for them."

"How come you know all of this, Robert? Why would Mr. Halifax make you his confidante?"

"You mean since I'm only a driver, his employee, why would he trust me? That I'm not trustworthy? No, no, don't shake you head. I know that's what you think. That's all right. I understand. But who else was he going to tell? His wife? His other sons? His accountants? He needed some help and I was there, ready to give it to him. And now Lila will be all alone. . ."

"Robert, can you prove you were in New York that day Mr. Halifax died?" *I believe Robert's story. Unfortunately it doesn't help Manny at all.*

"Yes, of course. Lila will tell you. Her mother will confirm it. Here. Give me a piece of paper. I'll give you her number." I fish a piece of paper out of my handbag, hand it to him and he quickly jots down a number. "This is her phone number. Go call her."

And so I do. On my cellular phone. A soft, feminine, sweet voice answers.

"Is this Lila Hamilton?" I ask.

"It is."

"This is Sergant Wilkins, Montgomery County Maryland Police. Ms. Hamilton, we're investigating Mr. Halifax's murder."

"Oh my God."

"Ms. Hamilton, we're talking to all of Mr. Halifax's employees. One of them claims to have been in New York with you on October 6, the day of the murder. Can you identify who that was?"

"I'll get him in trouble. Nobody knows he comes here."

"What's his name, Ms. Hamilton. You must identify him. Whoever doesn't have an alibi for that day is under suspicion as a possible murderer and is going to be in deep trouble."

"His name is Robert Verona."

"Thank you, Ms. Hamilton. We'll be in touch if we need anything else."

I hang up and put the phone back in my bag. I pull out the ledger sheet and hand it to Robert.

"Thank you," is all he says.

I see my message light blinking when I get home.

"Gloria, it's Peter. Haven't heard from you. Call me." *Blip.*

A second message: "Gloria, honey, why haven't you called? Your father and I worry about you, you know. Would it be too much trouble for you to pick up the phone once in a while and tell us you're alive?"

I'm drained. I pour myself a glass of white wine and dial my parents' number.

One of Bach's violin concertos is playing on my CD player. The second movement. Its incredibly beautiful, ethereal melody washes over my soul. Such haunting sadness, such intense drama: the violin seems to be weeping. It stirs such deep emotions in me, so much sorrow for the passions I feel but can't quell.

17

Peter has been in my thoughts all day. I didn't call him last night. I still feel hurt that he didn't spend the weekend with me and that he gazed at Jenna with such obvious warmth. But I have him on my mind. I can't displace him from my heart. I miss his voice and I miss his presence.

Dinner is in the oven, a nice pot roast for me and Sue that should last me a couple of days. I put two glasses of wine on the table. Sue is in an expansive mood.

"Well, we finally get together, friend. Let's have a toast to friendship."

"You look very happy, Sue. It's great to see you like this."

"Well, it's love, friend. Pure and simple. Love." *I wish she would stop calling me "friend."* "Did I tell you that Ron is a great lover? I mean he is great!"

"No, I don't think you said anything like that to me."

She's not paying any attention to what I'm saying.

"Perfect. Just perfect," she croons. "He knows what and where, if you know what I mean."

"Sure I know." *Sure I know.*

"Would you like to hear some of the details?"

"Maybe later, after dinner." I really don't want to hear the details of Sue's love life. I wouldn't know how to respond.

"Well, let me just tell you that he's a marvelous lover. I hope it'll last. He hasn't said anything about love yet, but I hope that comes soon. Let's eat. When's the food going to be ready? I'm starving. I haven't eaten anything in ages." I serve the roast, some home-fried potatoes, and a loaf of French bread I picked up on my way home. We clink glasses.

"*Salud,*" she says. "This smells heavenly." She digs into the roast with great enthusiasm. I smile.

"Sue, your affair with Halifax, how long did it last?" I need to broach the subject of Lila and Donny.

"Who cares? I don't remember any more. I want to concentrate on the here and now. Hey, Gloria, this is a great roast."

"Sue," the words get stuck in my throat. "Sue. . ."

"Well, out with it, girl. What is it you want to know? You've been stumbling and stammering all evening. What's bothering you?"

"Do you have a sister named Lila?" The words come out of my mouth in a rush.

Sue becomes very pale. The fork in her hand is suspended in mid-air. I can hear the short spurts of air she releases through her open lips. She purses them in a mocking expres-

sion and finally lets out a small, strident laugh.

"Well. So you know."

"Tell me about her."

"She's young and beautiful. She stole the man I was sleep-
ing with, fucked him and got pregnant. Now she has a small
child who could one day develop a horrible disease. I have
nothing to do with her. Nothing at all." Her eyes are shiny,
brimming with tears.

"Have you seen the baby?"

"Yeah. Once or twice, when I was in New York. My mother takes care of him. I went to see them while Lila was at
work."

"Is he O.K.?"

"I guess. I don't know. I don't ask and I don't care. Why
the hell are you asking me all this?"

"Because I'm trying to find out what happened to Mr.
Halifax."

"And you think that sweet little Lila had anything to do
with it? She was in love with him. The idiot. I'll tell you what
happened to Halifax. Manny killed him. That's what happened."

"I don't think Manny did it, Sue. I really believe he's
innocent."

Sue brushes the hair off her face which is slightly flushed
after the dinner and wine. She looks warm in the gray business suit she wore at the office. She takes off her jacket and
opens the first three buttons of her pale blue silk shirt. She
fans her bosom with her open palm. She's not interested in
Manny. She's not concerned about him. All at once Sue

appears different to me. The warmth of her personality seems contrived, her smile looks false, her gestures and voice and stance seem hollow. She frequently claims she loves each one of us, that she cares deeply for her staff. I once believed all that. But she has done nothing that I know of to help Manny. Even though she's the one who brought him here from KMEX, Halifax's station in L.A., to put him on WVVV in D.C. She had promised him stardom at the station. She called him her star pupil when his ratings began to soar. And she seemed to care about him genuinely.

"Look," she says, "the police think he did it. He threatened old Vince. He's hot tempered, he was mad as hell and he killed the old guy. There isn't much more than that."

A few moments later, she breezily picks up her jacket, pats me on the head and says: "It was real good, kid. We'll have to do it again sometime. Soon."

It was a truly unpleasant evening. As soon as Sue leaves I reach for the phone. I need to hear Peter's voice.

"Yes?" His voice sounds wonderfully masculine.

"Peter, it's Gloria. Are you alone?"

"Yes, I am. I've been calling you. Where have you been?"

I'd like to invite him to come over, but its after midnight. It's not a great idea.

"I met with Verona last night."

"You did what? Where? Gloria, that was very foolish. He might be a very dangerous man. He could be a murderer." *Is that concern I hear in his voice?* "Were you alone?"

"Yes. I was alone."

"Gloria, why?"

"I returned the ledger to him."

"What? Oh no! Why did you do that? It'll never help us now, unless it's uncovered with a search warrant."

Please don't lecture me. I take the portable phone to the bedroom and start getting ready for bed. "He wasn't blackmailing Mr. Halifax," I say. "He was helping him in a love affair. He was taking the payments to the mother of Halifax's little bastard son."

"He told you that?"

"He did."

"And you believe him?"

"I do. I confirmed it with Halifax's lover."

Peter's tone has changed noticeably. He's mellower, more caressing. I lie down on the bed, pull up the covers, turn off the light, and place the phone very close to my face.

"Gloria, I hope you're doing the right thing. Jenna hasn't been able to get any relevant information from Manny. He hardly talks to her. I don't think he wants to be helped. I'm not sure she'll be able to pull him out of this. He's being extremely uncooperative."

"Peter. . ." I whisper into the phone. "Peter. . ."

"Yes, babe?"

"Peter, I don't know anymore. Sue thinks Manny's guilty. He swore to me he didn't rape anybody."

"He didn't have to force the girl in order for it to be considered rape. If he had sex with a minor, that's a sufficient offense."

"Peter, can we help him?"

"We'll sure try, babe. We'll sure try."

"I want to see you soon."

"I want to see you, too."

"I really would like to feel you close to me right now."

"How close?"

"Very, very close. My arms feel empty without you."

"You're a sweet, darling girl, Gloria. You make me feel so young and alive being around you."

"But Peter . . ."

"What, babe?"

"You don't understand." *I want you so much. I'm aching for you.*

"Keep talking to me, my sweet. The sound of your voice is so soothing."

"Peter. . ." *I would like to feel your lips on mine. I want your whole body pressed against me. I want to feel you caressing every part of my body.* "You're so dear to me."

I arch my back and stretch my legs. I bend them and embrace my pillow against my swollen breasts. "Oh, Peter. . ."

Walter is in the office today. I haven't seen him since the memorial service. He looks very dapper in a lime-green silk shirt, brown pants, Italian loafers with no socks. His shirt sleeves are rolled up to his elbows, his arms are tanned and muscular. I can hear his loud voice down the hallway of the station. He's joking, patting backs, and smiling jovially at everyone.

"Gloria, well, hello Gloria. You're certainly looking beautiful today. Quite fetching." I feel myself blush. He's a good looking man. "I need to ask you a big favor. Big. You know your contest about crimes?"

"Yes . . .?"

"I think I have a great idea. A magnificent idea. See if you like it. It occurred to me that if you use the setting of my gallery for one of your crimes, the gallery would get a lot of publicity. As a matter of fact, you can stage a murder-mystery right in the gallery. You could invite your better listeners, serve them some champagne, caviar, all my treat, you understand, and let them loose. Let 'em solve a crime. We could have a blast. And you would have it all on the air. Broadcast the whole thing live. And then give the winner a great art prize. Again, my treat. Doesn't it sound fabulous? What do you think?"

"Let me think about it, Walter." *Sure, that's all I need now, when I'm about to do something bold.*

"I've given this a lot of thought. Your show would get great ratings and my gallery would get a lot of publicity." He is smiling and winking at me throughout the whole presentation.

"Music fans, welcome to the 'Crime in the Afternoon Contest'." *Irma is going to be very mad I haven't called her for today's contest. I don't want to have her involved today. I have to pursue, in my own way, all the leads. Walter was not at the opening of his gallery. I have to find out where he was. I know that if my efforts fail today, I will certainly lose my job, and worse yet, Manny won't have anybody at the station who believes in him.*

"The topic of this afternoon's contest is a difficult one," I continue. "It deals with incest and murder. As, for example, when a stepson and a stepmother are having an affair. A rich stepson living in the same house with a beautiful young step-mother. They're crazy for each other. Perhaps here, in our midst, in Washington, D.C. Then the husband gets killed. And the stepson is not where he is supposed to be at the time of the murder. Who do you suppose might have killed the husband? It shouldn't be too hard to guess. I'll open up the phone lines shortly. First correct answer gets one thousand dollars on the spot."

The doors of the studio burst open. Walter is standing at the door glaring at me.

"How dare you? How dare you accuse me of incest and murder, you little bitch. It's me you're talking about, isn't it?" He's screaming. People are converging on the studio from all over the station. "You shut your mouth, you little bitch!"

"It's too late, Walter. The contest is on. The phones will start ringing very soon." I appear calm but I'm trembling inside. I pick up a CD and play it right after the commercial. "Besides," I add, "I have proof."

"What the hell are you talking about? Proof of what?"

"Of your affair with Irma."

"You're absolutely crazy," he sputters. "Totally crazy." "Whatever gave you the idea that I'm having an affair with Irma? She was my father's wife, for goodness sake." The whole staff of the station is standing at the studio door listening. Nobody says a word. Walter is livid. He walks toward me, lifts a marble award 'Thank you for you support from the March of Dimes' and raises it above his head. I don't move. I don't

186

even flinch. I'm trembling inside but I don't move a muscle. Nobody is stirring outside the studio doors either. All of a sudden, Drew pushes the crowd aside and rushes into the studio, standing next to Walter facing me.

"Will you tell me what you're doing, Gloria?" he demands.

"She's lost her mind!" Walter exclaims.

"Drew," I say, "Walter and Irma may be the ones who killed Mr. Halifax. Irma has a diary with detailed descriptions of her affair with Walter." Walter starts to protest, but I go on. "In addition, Walter was not at the gallery opening the day his father was killed."

"I was there, you malicious twit."

"Not when Sue was there."

Sue has walked into the studio and is observing the scene very quietly.

"That's true, Walter. You weren't there. I left after seven o'clock and you still weren't there." *Thank you, Sue. I owe you one.*

"I arrived later."

"Sure," I pipe in a shrill, unnatural voice, "after you killed your father."

"Tell her, Walter." Drew says. *What does Drew know about this?*

"No."

"Tell her or I will." Drew is being more forceful.

"It will ruin you and your marriage."

I'm speechless. I turn around and insert another CD. The whole staff is still standing in the hallway outside the studio.

Nobody is making a sound. The only thing you can hear are the soft sounds of Ella Fitzgerald singing 'The Man I Love.'

An eerie quiet surrounds us.

Walter and Drew are staring at each other. Very slowly, Drew reaches out, removes the marble award from Walter's hand, lays it carefully on the console next to me, takes hold of Walter's shoulders and says, "Walter arrived late to the opening because he was with me. We're lovers."

I call Peter as soon as I get home to tell him about my encounter with Walter. I'm astonished at Drew's revelation, I'm sure everybody at the station is. I feel in need of a shoulder to lean on. A friendly face. I don't know whether I still have a job. My ploy to trap Walter has the entire staff in an uproar and Sue didn't say one single word to me all evening. She had left the station before I finished my shift.

Peter says he'll join me for dinner at Max's Bar and Grill after a meeting with the Ethics Committee of the D.C. Bar. He's a newly elected member and he's proud to be serving there. I get there early and wait for him. This has become our place. Small, cozy, dark, quiet. I'm sipping a glass of wine, worried about my job, sad about Manny, and happy I'm going to see Peter. The moment he walks through the door, with his quick pace, his scarf flying behind him, his hair a bit disheveled, his tilted smile, my heart quickens. My palms get moist. I have to bite my lower lip so that he doesn't notice how it quivers with excitement at the mere sight of him.

"Peter, I really need to ask you something," I say when he's settled at the table. "It's been bothering me. It's really not my business but I need to know."

"Go ahead and ask, kiddo. I don't have too many secrets from you." The waiter brings him a beer.

"I bet."

He smiles, orders a hamburger, medium rare, and reaches for one of my cold french fries.

"So, what has been bothering you?"

"If you don't want to answer, I'll understand," I say.

"Gloria, for goodness sake, ask me." He gulps down his beer.

"Where were you last weekend? I . . . thought perhaps we would spend some of it together." I avoid his eyes. He doesn't owe me any explanations.

"I see. Well, it's a family matter." He looks away.

"I'm sorry. I really shouldn't intrude."

"It's O.K. My father is in a nursing home in Baltimore. He's very sick and very old. They called me Saturday evening–he'd taken a turn for the worse."

"I'm sorry."

"Right after moot court I left to see him. To be with him. He didn't even recognize me. . ."

I don't want to hear any more. I regret I caused Peter pain just thinking about it. I don't even feel like biting into my hamburger. I feel that would be intruding into his sadness.

"After I left the nursing home I was so depressed, I decided to stay over in Baltimore and spend all Sunday with him. I don't know how much time he has left."

"Peter, I'm sorry I asked."

"It's all right. I want to tell you. I want you to know

what's happening in my life. What is interesting, however, is that I took a room at the Sheraton at the Inner Harbor and decided to go to the bar for a sandwich and a nightcap before going to bed. Interesting thing happened, I might as well tell you. You might get a kick out of it. You know that Karl Sconix is representing that girl accusing Manny of rape, right?"

"Yes."

"Well, Sconix is some character, I'll tell you. Quite unsavory. He's been involved in a few shady deals, has been investigated by my committee more than once. Nothing concrete to pin on him, though. Ever met him?"

"No, I don't think so."

"He's married to a very wealthy older woman. She comes from a family that sells diamonds. Really loaded. Sconix lives very well. But word has it his wife has him on a very short leash. Anyway, here I go to get a bite to eat, sitting by myself at the Sheraton bar, and right behind me I hear a familiar voice. I turn around and it's none other than Karl Sconix in an extremely compromising position with a young blond with very big breasts and a very low-cut blouse. I finished my sandwich and my drink, got up, walked over to Karl and said, 'Good seeing you Karl. I hope you and your adorable companion have a delectable evening.' Then I turned and walked away."

I'm giggling. So is Peter. We double up with laughter.

When we subside, I bite into my juicy hamburger. Peter does the same.

18

I still have a job. Sue called me into her office today as soon as I walked in. I was expecting the worst. She was very stern. No more "friend." Now it was plain "Gloria, listen to me." If I promise to stay out of trouble, if I "keep my nose clean and do what you're supposed to do and stay out of other peoples's business" I could keep my job. I promised right away. I'm sorry I have to break my promise almost immediately. What I've got to do now is meet with the girl who accused Manny–Julia Reynosa is her name, I think–and her mother. I have to hear directly from her that Manny violated her. I will not believe it any other way.

"Peter, it's Gloria. Hi. You very busy?"

"I'm preparing for a class I have to teach in fifteen minutes. Why?"

"We need to get Julia Reynosa's address. The girl who

accused Manny. We absolutely have to talk to her."

"Why are you calling me about it?"

"You know Sconix. Get the address from him. I'm sure he has it. He has to have it. Threaten him if necessary. Tell him you're going to expose him for cheating on his wife."

"Gloria, what's the matter with you? You know I can't do that. It's unethical. Besides, we're probably wasting our time. Jenna believes that Manny actually had sex with the girl."

"Peter, Jenna is very nice. A lovely woman." *I have to choose my words carefully here. I think Peter really likes Jenna.* "But she doesn't believe in Manny. Besides, she's probably getting paid very little, since Manny doesn't have much money."

"She's doing it pro bono. For free. As a favor to me."

"There, you see, she doesn't . . ."

"Gloria," he says seriously, "she's an advocate. Whether or not she's paid, she'll do the best job she's capable of. And Manny is lucky to have her. She's a very good lawyer. Very good." *Ouch, sore point. Next topic. Fast.*

"I'm sorry. I didn't mean anything by that. But please, try to get Julia's address. That's all you need to do. I'll do the rest. I promise."

"Look, come with me to the D.C. bar meeting tonight. Karl goes there sometimes. If he's there, I'll introduce you to him. You ask him. Got to run. Meet me at the law school right after your shift."

My shift was surprisingly good. My crazy fan hasn't called me since Verona plastered him. My contest has attracted a nice following and my cues were close to perfect. Besides, I'm about to pick up Peter. I'm driving and smiling and listening to the classical music station.

Since Drew replaced Manny with a ho-hum deejay he stole from a competing station, I no longer listen to the "Love Songs" program. It has no spark. No life. I'm humming along with a lilting Strauss waltz.

Peter's waiting for me outside the law school. He's wearing a gray business suit, a white shirt and a striped gray and blue tie. Very dapper. He slides into the passenger seat of my little blue Escort and lightly pecks my cheek. I close my eyes and inhale his cologne. I reach over and caress his cheek.

"This is the plan," he admonishes me gently. "I'll introduce you to Sconix and stand next to you. You ask him only about the girl's address. Nothing more. Agreed?"

"Sure."

"Gloria?"

"Yes, of course. Agreed."

It's a half-hour drive to downtown Washington, to the building where the D.C. bar meets. I park in a parking lot, grab Peter's arm and skip to his fast pace. We enter a large hall filled with people. All lawyers, Peter says. A quick glance around the room and he spots Sconix standing by the bar.

"Come, let's go, Gloria. We don't have much time. Karl, hi there. This is Gloria Berk, she's been wanting to meet you."

"Mr. Sconix, such a pleasure." I'm staring into the brown eyes of a short, slim man. Lively, dancing eyes. His hair is graying. He needs a shave. His expensive-looking dark brown suit is rumpled a bit, his brown silk tie askew. I extend my hand and he shakes it warmly. He has a most attractive smile.

"I've wanted to meet you for a while now," I say. His smiles becomes wider, the handshake warmer. "You're very famous around our station, you know, Mr. Sconix." He still has my hand.

"That's very flattering, Gloria. Please call me Karl. And what station is that?"

"WVVV." The smile fades away instantly. He lets my hand drop.

"And what do you do there?" The tone is icy.

"I'm a deejay. On the air in the afternoons. I'm also in charge of the women's committee of the station."

"The what?"

Peter is moving closer to me and I can tell he's listening intently. He grasps my arm. *Are you getting nervous, Peter, dear? Am I making you a bit nervous?*

"You see, we've had some cases of sexual harassment at the station . . . "

"Gloria . . . " Peter interrupts sharply.

"It's O.K., Peter. I'm sure I can trust Karl here with this information. It's not happening anymore but I think that all of us women must be aware of it. Don't you agree? So, I'm putting together a pamphlet with some ideas, some stories, and examples, so my co-workers can recognize it when it's staring them in the face. Good idea, don't you think, Karl?" I'm flirting shamelessly with him, touching his arm, moving my hips, licking my lips.

"Gloria, did you have a question for Karl? We need to get going to the meeting."

"Well, I'd like to interview you," I say, "when there's a little more time. I'm sure a famous attorney like you would be able to relate dozens of interesting cases. I could even interview you on the air sometime. You'd like that, wouldn't you?" He's smiling again, relaxing a bit. "I'm sure you'd be great," I continue. "Really great." *It's time to broach the subject. Now.* "Also, I'd like to write a small piece on the girl who was sexually harassed by Manny Miranda." I can't bring myself to say raped. "I need her address."

"I'm afraid I can't divulge that kind of information." The bantering is definitely over.

"If she doesn't want to talk to me, I won't force the issue, I promise." I move closer to him.

"I can't give you that information. Sorry." He starts moving away. I look pleadingly at Peter. He's avoiding my stare. He's looking away. Finally he stares at Sconix, leans toward him and whispers something. I strain to hear, but the din of all the lawyers milling and talking makes it impossible. The only thing I can hear is, "O.K., Peter. O.K. you win." Sconix takes out a blank card from his black alligator briefcase, quickly scribbles something, and roughly shoves the card into my hand. "Don't tell them who gave it to you." He strides off and is quickly lost in the crowd.

"Did you mention the blonde?"

Peter smiles, pats my arm, and walks away.

This is the first time I've seen Manny since his arrest. He's gaunt and pale, almost yellow. His normally slender features have a hollow cast. He has dark circles under his eyes. I can clearly see his protruding cheekbones.

"Do you mind if I smoke?" he asks but doesn't wait for an answer. He pulls out a cigarette. His hands are trembling; I avert my eyes so he doesn't realize that I've noticed. But he does. He can hardly light his cigarette. I get up from the love seat, approach the couch where he's sitting, and hold the lighter steady for him. He pulls in the flame, blows out the smoke very slowly, and stretches out his long legs.

"Thanks, Gloria. It's good to see you. I feel I have no friends left except for you. I haven't told my parents about any of this. I don't even want to think what all this is going to do to them." He leans his head back and closes his eyes. I'm still standing close to him. I want to touch him, give him some of my strength; he looks so defeated. He also hasn't shaved in what must be several days.

"Manny, can I get you something to drink?"

"No. When will your friend be here?"

"I expect Peter around ten-thirty or eleven. He's at a D.C. bar meeting." I pour some white wine into two glasses and lay them gently on the coffee table, close to Manny.

"Are you hungry?"

"I don't know. I don't think I've eaten much in several days."

"I can tell. Let me fix you something."

"Gloria, how did I land in so much trouble?" he asks. "I haven't done anything. What's happening to me?" He takes a drag on a cigarette with his eyes half-closed. His long eyelashes cast sinuous shadows over his cheeks. His lips are partly open and his chest is rising methodically as he breathes. He's an incredibly beautiful man. I love to have him here. *My God, how selfish can I be? He's here only because he's in trouble.* But I love to have him here. His presence. His hands. His voice.

"I'm sure Peter and Jenna will help you," I say as soothingly as I can. "Everything's going to get straightened out. You'll see." I'm preparing a platter of ham and cheese. Also, I put the coffee machine on. I know Peter will want some coffee when he comes in.

"Have you met Jenna?" he asks.

"Yes."

"What do you think of her?"

"I don't know, Manny. She seems smart. Peter says she's very good."

"She doesn't believe me. She doesn't believe I didn't kill Halifax."

"Manny, did you . . . ?"

The bell rings and my heart skips a beat. I hurry to let Peter in. He brings in the softness of the moonlight outside. He brings in lightness and music and smiles. *If I could just rush to you and hug you and kiss you hello.*

"Peter," I shake his hand, "please come in." I take his coat. "Have you met Manny?"

Manny stands up to greet Peter. He looms over Peter. But Peter's athletic frame looks sturdy and strong. The two of them are standing in the middle of my living room, staring at each other, without moving or talking. It must be just a second or two, but the hush is complete. I'm standing by the doorway holding Peter's coat in my arm, astonished at the sight of the two men in their silent, static, manly dance. At

197

last Peter breaks the spell, reaches out and grabs Manny's limp hand. "It's a pleasure," he says. He turns to me. "Gloria, got some coffee around here?"

Peter takes the cup of coffee from my hand, grazing my fingers. He sits close to Manny, looks straight into his eye and says:

"Tell me the whole story, Manny. Let's see what we can do."

Manny is silent. He looks forlorn and desperate. He covers his face with his long fingers and lets out a loud sob.

Peter places his arm around Manny's convulsing shoulders. "We're going to try, Manny. It's going to be O.K."

A cool, sunny Saturday afternoon. I've set up a time for Monday evening when Peter, Manny, and I can go talk to Julia Reynosa and her mother. This afternoon I'm taking a break from that. I'm having lunch with Steve. He called last night and we decided to "start this friendship all over again."

The pale golden light of the fall sun is pouring into my apartment, making the mirror shimmer in myriad tones of orange, bronze, and lemon. I throw open the doors to my small balcony to let the brisk fresh air waft in. It carries the scents of coffee, candied apples, and pumpkin pie. It's so cool outside that even Honey–the neighbor's cat, napping on my balcony–looks as though her fur coat is too thin to keep her warm. The place feels so cool, so fresh it makes me feel, as I walk through it, that I'm bathing in a silvery spring.

My heart and my thoughts are filled with Peter, his tanned strong hands, his sculpted neck, his beautiful warm smile.

A few drops of light cologne behind my ears, a quick check in the mirror, and I'm ready to go. Peter has been good for my soul. I smile a little as I gaze at myself. I look quite good. Shiny hair and eyes. My lips look somewhat fuller than usual. Even my breasts look rounder in the red turtleneck I'm wearing. I know my mother would approve. "Women ought to look like women," she says, "not broomsticks."

As soon as I close the balcony doors and grab my jacket from the chair, the phone rings.

"Yes?" I sing into the phone.

"You thought your tough boyfriend would scare me? You thought you could get rid of me so easily? You damn bitch!"

Not him again. Please God.

"Why are you doing this? What do you want?"

"You, my little pussy."

"Can you please leave me alone?"

"As long as you cavort with other men, I'll be there. Looking at you. Listening to you. Following you. Don't you forget it."

I hang up the phone as hard as I can, grab my jacket, and trot down the stairs. Perry's Restaurant is just down the block from me. Running all the way, I arrive breathless and annoyed that this Saturday afternoon's magic has evaporated.

We sit on the rooftop gardens at Perry's. Despite the cold. We're the only ones sitting here. I'm sure our waiter won't be thrilled to climb all the way up here to bring us our sushi and green tea, but the view is so sweeping, so grand, that Steve insisted we brace the cold and "take it like good little soldiers." From where I'm sitting, I can clearly see the glittering top of the National Cathedral and the swaying tree tops of Rock Creek Park. I feel as if I'm perched on one of those trees.

Steve looks at me as I warm my hands on my tea cup. "You look stunning, Gloria. What have you done to yourself?" *Is that supposed to be a compliment?* "You're just beautiful. I feel like an ass the way I drove the other night. I must've scared the hell out of you."

"Yeah. It was a little scary."

"Was that professor Wilson in the car with you?"

"Yes, it was."

"Oh, I see," he says taking hold of my freezing hand. "Can he stand a little competition? Can I still try to win you over?"

"It's a free country." I laugh.

"Are you very cold?"

"Not very. Why? Do I look cold? Am I turning blue?"

"No. But you're shaking."

"Oh. It's not the cold."

"What, then? The nearness of me?"

"Cute, Steve. Very cute." I pat his hand. *It's time to confess. It's time to open up to someone. Now. And who better than a friendly policeman?*

I tell him my story about the crazy fan. The phone calls. My fears. I end up with an apologetic laugh. "That's all it is. Nothing much."

"This isn't a laughing matter, Gloria. There are psychos everywhere. And they can be dangerous. I don't like it one bit. You've got to be careful. Especially an attractive girl like you. Out in the public eye. You should've contacted the authorities earlier. Call me the next time it happens here." He hands me a card with his pager number on it. "I've punched in all your phone numbers, so I'll know it's you. We'll catch him, I promise."

"Thank's, Steve. I appreciate it." *I hope there's no 'next time.'*

Steve walks me home. "It's the least I can do for a friend," he says, taking hold of my arm. I don't pull away. I wonder how he looks in his police uniform. His broad shoulders and strong arms must make him look very powerful. As we walk past the corner cigar store, I peek in. A dark figure with copper-colored hair is leaning against the glass door. My heart takes a tumble.

Steve notices. "You O.K.?" he asks. "Is everything allright"

"I'm fine. I guess I'm a little jumpy."

We stop by the door of my building. "Can I come up?" he asks.

"Another time. I'm busy this evening."

"Seeing the professor?"

"No, not really." *Don't I wish.*

Steve places both arms on the door frame, looks down at me and kisses my forehead. "Call me when you're ready for more," he says. "Meantime, be careful."

The moment I walk into my apartment there's a knock on the door, I smile. I had a feeling Steve wasn't going to take no for an answer that easily.

"All right," I call out, "you win." I peek through the peep-hole. *My God.* I exhale loudly. My legs start to tremble. The stalker is standing outside my door!

"Open up, Gloria," he demands. He starts to knock harder. "Come on, let me in. I only want to talk to you."

I want to run away, but there's no escape. I have to keep him here so Steve can nab him. But I don't want this man to know I'm about to call the police, or he'll flee the coop.

"What do you want with me?" I whisper through the closed door. I see him come closer to the door to hear me. "Why don't you leave me alone?"

"Let me in."

"First tell me what you want. Tell me." I'm growing bolder. My voice is getting louder. "You want to look at me?" I'm fairly shouting now, as I start walking to the phone in the living room. "You want to find somebody to love you? To make love to you?" I'm dialing Steve's pager number. "You think I could possibly enjoy making love to you?"

I tiptoe back to the door. He's still standing out there. A crazed smile bares his dirty, ugly teeth.

He starts to turn around. I think he realizes what I just did. I need to keep him here for just a few more minutes.

I put the chain on my door and slowly open it a few inches. "What's your name?" I ask in a mild tone.

He turns around. "Oscar, my name's Oscar."

"Oscar," I whisper. I don't know how to handle the situation. "Why don't you leave me alone?"

"I love you, Gloria. I love everything about you. Your voice, your hair, your life style. I want to make you love me back."

There are muffled footsteps on the staircase. The stalker lurches toward my door and pushes hard, ripping the chain from its bolts. His foul breath envelops me. His arms are grasping my shoulders.

"No, no," I cry out.

"Leave her alone," Steve shouts, running up the stairs. He comes up behind the guy, jerks his arms back and spins him around. In a few seconds the character is cuffed.

"You're under arrest. You have the right. . ."

I can barely close the door behind me, my hands are shaking so badly. Tears are streaming down my cheeks and I don't even bother to wipe them away. I walk to the window to see Steve shoving the stalker into his car. All of a sudden I feel very free and grateful to Steve. I glance up and catch a glimpse of the sun's fading rays over Adam's Morgan.

19

Julia Reynosa lives with her mother in a third-floor walk-up apartment off Columbia Road, in a Hispanic section of Adams Morgan. They're practically my neighbors—just across the avenue where the shops and the restaurants are. It's a crowded place, noisier than where I live. Also livelier. The Hispanic festival held here is famous all over the city. I attend every year. It's strange to be here now, without the exhilaration of the festival, of the mouth-watering aromas emanating from the food stalls, the intermingling sounds and rhythms of different Latin bands.

That's Julia and Amparo's neighborhood.

Manny and I are standing in front of the Reynosa apartment building, waiting for Peter to arrive. Manny is very nervous, but I notice him relax as soon as Peter joins us. I smile at him and he tousles my hair. We don't know whether we'll be able to talk to Julia. We're taking a chance we'll find her at home for dinner. We go in and climb the stairs. I knock softly on the door. In my hand is a bouquet of sunflowers and a box of chocolates. I didn't want to arrive empty-handed.

A thin, olive-skinned girl opens the door slightly. Manny stands behind Peter and me, but he's so much taller that he can't really hide.

"Julia?" I ask.

The big brown eyes examine me inquisitively. "Yes," she answers softly and timidly. She sees Manny and retreats a few paces. She can't be more than four feet-ten nor weigh more than ninety pounds. She wears her hair in braids, a blue satin ribbon at each end. Pretty girl. Very young.

"May we come in? Here, these are for you." I hand her the bouquet of sunflowers. They fairly cover her face. I show her the box of chocolates.

"I don't know." She eyes the box of chocolates.

"Here." I hand it to her. "These are also for you."

"Thank you."

"Is you mother home?" Peter asks softly.

"Who is it, Julia?" a thickly accented voice calls sharply from inside the apartment. "Who is it. . .?" She appears at the door. A bright red apron is tied around her black skirt. She has a broad lined face, small brown eyes, graying hair. She sees Manny and pales.

"Please, Mrs. Reynosa," Manny pleads in his softest, most caressing voice. "*Por favor,* please, let us in. I need to talk to Julia. If I did anything wrong, anything at all, I must apologize. *Por favor. Le ruego.* I'm begging. It doesn't matter to me that you'll sue the station or me. It doesn't matter if I lose my job. The only important thing here is if I did anything wrong anything at all, I must apologize to your daughter. Please let us come in."

Mrs. Reynosa is standing at the door, hands on her large hips, her short legs spread apart. Julia stands behind her, peering at us.

"I don't know. My lawyer, er, I mean Julia's lawyer has said we shouldn't talk to anyone."

"Mrs. Reynosa," Peter says with a smile, "I'm an attorney, too. I'm a friend of Mr. Sconix. He's aware that we're coming here. We're here to help Manny apologize to Julia." *Well, well, well. He surely picked up on Manny's idea. Not bad, Peter.* "After you hear him out, if you ask us to leave, I give you my solemn word, we'll leave right away."

Peter can be persuasive. Mrs. Reynosa opens the door.

"Just for a few minutes. I'm cleaning the dinner dishes and Julia needs to do her homework."

"We understand," Peter says, following her to their small living room. The furniture is old and very worn. A couch is in one corner with two mismatched chairs opposite, and a large old television blaring in another corner. Mrs. Reynosa walks over to the TV and turns the sound down a little. The Spanish-language station is showing what seems to be a soap opera. Mrs. Reynosa stands by the set and watches for a few seconds before turning back to us.

"Well, talk." She is standing in front of Manny, completely eclipsing Julia, who is sitting in one of the chairs, chewing on one of her braids. Her feet barely touch the worn gold carpet.

Manny hesitates. He's sitting on the couch, with Peter and I standing on either side of him like silent guards.

"Are you going to talk or do I go back to my kitchen?"

"Ma'am, Julia, please forgive . . . Julia, I never touched you. You came to see me with your friend that one evening. Do you remember? Do you remember, Julia? Julia, please look at me. Tell them, tell your mother. Did I ever touch you?" He's trying hard to get Julia to look at him.

"Julia, *Vete de aqui.* Now! *Ahora mismo.* Leave. Leave this instant." Mrs. Reynosa is screaming.

"No I won't." Julia says. "I want to stay. This concerns me." Finally, there is defiance in her voice. Her mother lifts her hand, as if to strike the girl.

"You talk like that to your mother?" she says. "How dare you, child?"

Julia cowers. Peter and I run over to Julia reflexively to protect her girl. Julia glances at her mother, then at Manny, and in a quiet, childish voice says, "Mamá, I have to stay. I want to talk. I want to tell the truth."

"The truth is that he raped you," the mother says. "He forced you to have oral sex with him."

"No, Mamá, that's not the truth! I don't want to hurt Manny. He's nice. I like him. He let me and Louisa into the studio when we asked him to. He's nice, Mamá. I like him very much. He was nice to me. To my friends."

Peter slowly walks over to Julia, bends down, kneels in front of her, takes her hands in his two own hands and gently urges, "Julia, please tell us exactly what happened. Manny's in a lot of trouble. Only you can help him. Only you." Julia's big eyes are downcast, staring at her feet. "Julia, please listen to me," he continues. "The life of a man, a good man, depends on you. Did he rape you? Did he make love to you? Did he touch you improperly?" Julia starts to sob.

"Yes he did!" the mother screams. "He did! We already told the lawyer. The Mrs. knows all about . . ."

"The Mrs.?" Peter springs to his feet and turns to her. I'm surprised at his agility. "The Mrs.? Who is the Mrs.?"

"I . . . I don't know. I just said it. It doesn't mean anything."

Peter's tone has changed. He's in court now. He's defending the life of his client. "Mrs. Reynosa, who is the Mrs.? If you've been lying, now is the time to tell the truth, because if this goes to court–because I'm telling you right now we're not going to settle this–if this goes to court and we show that you've been lying, I promise you, Mrs. Reynosa, you will surely end up in jail. I hope you understand me. And it won't be easy for Julia either."

"Mamá."

"*Silencio, niña.* Be quiet."

"Mamá, tell them."

Mrs. Reynosa is twisting her fingers, playing with her apron, looking forlornly around the room.

"Tell them, Mamá!"

I go over to Mrs. Reynosa, who is still standing in the middle of the room, and gently walk her to the couch. Sitting between her and Manny, I plead, "Tell us, Mrs. Reynosa. It will make it easier for everybody."

Amparo Reynosa leans forward, looks at Manny and whispers, "She hates you. She hates you so much she wanted to hurt you bad."

"Who, Mrs. Reynosa? Who hates Manny?" Peter insits. The gentleness has returned to his voice.

"She. The Mrs."

"Who is the Mrs.?" Peter is pressing, his voice rising.

She makes some kind of sound and then blurts out, "Mrs. Halifax."

"Oh God." Manny lets out a groan. "Why would she do this to me? Why?"

"She didn't say. She came to me and Julia and say if we do this we make a lot of money."

"Mamá, tell them the whole story. Please, Mamá. Don't be afraid." Julia goes over to her mother, perches herself on the arm of the sofa, and puts a thin arm around her mother's shoulders.

"The Mrs. knows something bad about me. She swore she'd go to the police if we don't do this."

"Amparo, Mrs. Reynosa, what does she know about you?" Peter urges her. "I'm an attorney. Maybe I can help."

"I'm here not legal. The Mrs. knows it. She threatened me and said Julia will have to stay here by herself if they send me back to Mexico. I want a good life for Julia. I don't want to leave my little girl behind." She dabs her eyes with the hem of her apron.

"How come Mrs. Halifax knows you, Mrs. Reynosa?" Peter asks.

"I worked in a hotel in Mexico with her mother, Maria Elena. We were friends. Maria Elena came to visit the Mrs. here in Washington and I went to see her at the Mrs. house. I took Julia with me and the Mrs. met us there. Then she came to see us here about two weeks ago. With that attorney. They promised us a lot of money and also to help me get my green card. I believe them. I'm sorry we hurt you, Manny. *Lo siento tanto.* I'm sorry!"

Julia gets up, walks over to Manny, twines her small hands around his neck and sobs.

"Now you believe me, right? Now you know I'm innocent. I'm totally innocent. I didn't rape Julia–I didn't kill Mr. Halifax. You've got to believe me."

We're sitting in my apartment–Peter, Manny, and I. It's been a long day. We walked back from the Reynosa's apartment. It's just a few blocks and it's not too cold outside. We're all hungry, so we stopped and bought some Chinese take-out food on the way home. Now we're seated around my small dining table facing the balcony, with the food open before us. The sweet-smelling flowers–the ones that smell like jasmine–have dried; there was a frost two days ago and all the flowers have disappeared. I'm sitting close to Peter, almost touching him, Manny seated across from me. He seems relieved, happier, I think, more talkative. He's eating moo-shoo pork with great appetite. It makes me smile to see him eat with such enthusiasm. He's talking to us while taking enormous mouthfuls.

"Do you believe me Peter, do you?"

"Manny, take it easy. Let's analyze it one step at a time."

"But you know I didn't rape Julia. She told you that."

"Right, now your problem is not the rape. It's the murder charge."

I get up to fetch a bottle of wine. It's good to have Peter and Manny here. It's good to see them talking to each other. The atmosphere is warm, friendly, almost happy. I think Peter is starting to believe in Manny and Manny realizes it. He's grateful. So am I. I'm standing at my little kitchen counter, looking at the two of them, involved in their discussion, eating huge portions, their faces shimmering in the orange light from the fireplace flames. The scene makes me forget, for a second, that Manny is accused of murder. I return to the dining room with a bottle of wine. For a few moments I stand behind Peter, just to feel his essence. I put my hand on the nape of his neck and caress the hair closest to his neck. It's silky, fresh to my touch. He takes my hand and moves it across his face, pressing the palm to his lips. He leaves it there for a second or two. Manny looks up and watches us. He smiles. I think he understands my passion for Peter.

"Manny, there's evidence against you. Why haven't you helped Jenna?" Peter asks. "Don't you want her to defend you? Do you want another lawyer?"

Manny is quiet for a long time. "No, Jenna's fine. I guess she's a good lawyer. I don't know. I just don't think she understands. There's nothing she can do. There's nothing anybody can do to help me. Nothing I can do. Somebody set me up but I can't prove it."

"Were you at the Halifax estate the night of the murder?"

"I don't . . . I can't talk about it."

211

I feel a lump in my throat. He's not denying he was there. I expected him to deny it vehemently. "You couldn't have been there, Manny, you were at the studio with me . . ."

"It's no use, Gloria. Thank you, you're a good friend, but you know I wasn't there for at least an hour and a half."

"I know, I know," I insist. "But you had some emergency to take care of. You told me that. Don't you remember? Manny?"

"Gloria, let him explain in his own words where he was." Peter's voice is stern. I move slightly away from him. I need to protect Manny, his freedom, his integrity.

"Manny, where were you that evening?" Peter urges him. "Was it a woman? A man? Please tell us."

Manny pushes his chair back, and slowly raises his lean long body to its full height. He starts pacing my tiny living room. He looks like a caged panther. Flowing black shiny hair, bright furious eyes, strong muscles in his neck. His jaws are clenched, his fists closed tightly. I'm afraid of what's coming.

"I. . . I. . . She set me up. I was there that night."

Oh, my God, no. My friend. How can it be? "Manny. . ."

"Let him talk, babe." Peter takes my hand and holds it in both of his. "Let him talk."

"You won't believe me anyway."

"Try us, Manny. Where were you that evening?" Peter's voice is seductive.

"I was there."

"No, Manny." *I don't want him to confess. I don't want to hear what he's about to say.*

"Gloria, my good friend. It's true. I was there that night."

I run to Manny. "Why Manny, why did you go there? Did you kill Mr. Halifax?"

He looks down at me, takes my tear-stained face in his hands, and gently wipes my tears away. "I didn't kill him," he says softly. "I swear to you in my mother's name, I didn't. I didn't even see him there. I didn't see anybody at all."

I sob as he holds me quietly. Peter walks over to Manny, takes him by the shoulders and gently guides him to the couch.

"Sit down," he says. "Relax. Tell us the whole story. We'll help you. We'll do everything we can to get you out of this." *God bless you, my darling Peter.*

"But it really looks bad for me." Manny is talking very softly. "That's why I was reluctant to tell Jenna."

"Tell us, Manny," Peter coaxes.

I pour Manny a glass of wine. He takes it but doesn't drink.

"Irma came to talk to me in the station that Monday afternoon, the day Mr. Halifax was killed. It was during your shift, Gloria. She walked into my cubicle and sat in the chair by my desk. She was playful, touching my hand, caressing my thigh, laughing out loud. I didn't want people at the station to get the wrong impression. You know how gossip spreads there, and with my problems with Julia's accusations and Mr. Halifax being so angry with me, I didn't want to start any more rumors."

"I understand," I say. "So what did you do?"

"I was blunt with her and just asked her right off what I could do for her, so that she would leave my cubicle. "

"What did she say?" Peter is very interested.

"She just laughed. She said I couldn't do anything for her but that she could help me. That she knew Sconix, that if I went to her house that evening she would discuss my options with me."

"So you went?"

"I went. I didn't think I had an alternative. My job was on the line, my reputation. I really thought she was offering me help. So I told her I would see her there. She wanted me there by six o'clock. She said we would be alone, that Lucia would be in church and Walter would be at his opening. She added that Mr. Halifax would be out of town. She told me she would meet me there after her Detective Sabrina segment. She would leave the door open for me, I should walk in and she would greet me inside."

"So you went there alone?" I ask.

"Yes, I had to. I had no alternative. Did I, Peter?" He looks imploringly at Peter, who merely shakes his head. "I thought that if I went she would help me. I even thought of bringing her a peace offering. I stopped at Johnson's Flower Shop close to the station and bought her some red roses. You know where that is, Gloria?" I nod. "I wanted to offer them to her as a gesture of friendship. You know how she's been following me. She hounds me. During that cocktail party at her home she kept pressing her body to mine. In front of Mr. Halifax. When I said goodbye, she grabbed me by the neck and pulled me to her mouth. She kissed me long and hard in front of all the guests. Everybody saw it. It was embarrassing. But I couldn't pull away. Since I didn't respond to her overtures, she was angry with me. I even thought, as I drove over to her house, that if this was all a ploy to get me to make love to her, well. . ."

"I see." I want to change the topic immediately.

"What happened, Manny?" Peter is more patient than I.

"That's the puzzle. I got there at six, just like she asked me to. The door was open, like she said it would be. I walked in a few steps. The light in the foyer was on. I called her name several times from the entrance hall. Nobody answered. There was total silence in that big house. I walked a few more steps toward the living room. I tried to be very quiet. I didn't want to create a commotion. I didn't know if anybody else was there. I waited around for more than a half-hour and finally decided to leave. I felt shaky and my mouth was dry. So I first went to the kitchen and drank a glass of water. Then I left the house and returned to the station. She wasn't there, Peter. She just wasn't there."

"Did you tell any of this to the police?"

"I did. Over and over. They didn't believe me. They just laughed at me."

I'm outraged. "They laughed because your story lacked credibility?"

"Well . . . well . . . I can't tell you . . ."

"Manny," Peter stands up and starts pacing. "I need to know the whole truth here. This is no time to play coy. Come out with it! Everything!"

Manny hesitates for a moment or two and then blurts out, "Because I have a record, Peter. The police knew it and they threw it at me." Manny's voice is rising. His anger comes through his blazing eyes.

I'm speechless. I'm listening to Manny and don't recognize the man I thought I knew so well.

"What record?" Peter is also surprised.

"As a teenager, man. I belonged to a gang. Hell, everybody I knew in L.A. belonged to a gang in those days. We called ourselves *'Los gatos valientes.'* The brave cats. Man. We were supposed to defend the Hispanic businesses. It was tough for them. I think it still is. We got into more fights than I want to remember."

"What happened? Anybody got hurt?"

"No. Nobody got really hurt. But some members of the gang were caught stealing. Knives. Stealing knives. Can you believe it? They arrested all of us. All the members of the brave cats. It nearly killed my poor mother. Jesus. I swore I would make it up to her. To lead a good, Christian life. I thought that arrest would never come out, man. And now this. What am I going to do?"

Peter walks over to him calmly and says he doesn't know, but he sure as hell is going to help. He tells Manny he'll drive him home; he should try to get some rest. On their way out, Peter tells me that he'll stay with Manny until he's calmer.

I kiss Manny's cheek goodby and run my fingers over Peter's lips. I lean against the door listening to their fading footsteps.

The phone rings at about 1 a.m. It's Peter. He just got home. I'm in bed and feel happy he called.

"I stayed at Manny's apartment for about an hour," he says. He seems a little calmer."

"You're a good man. You know that Peter?" *And I just adore you.*

"Thank you, babe. You're not too bad yourself."

"Do you believe Manny?"

"I'm not sure. He knows there's evidence against him. It could be just a story, you know, about Irma inviting him to her house."

"We can check with the florist. See if they have a record that he really bought those roses."

"Yes, it might help."

"Peter . . ."

"Yes?"

"I like working with you."

He laughs. A warm, resonant laugh.

"I like working with you, too." He lets out a yawn.

"You're tired."

"Very."

"So am I." *But not enough to stop wanting you close to me. Holding me. I want your mouth. Your lips. Your arms.*

"I'll see you tomorrow in class, babe."

"I'm not really ready. I haven't studied much lately."

"Don't worry. I won't call on you."

"Peter . . ."

"Yes, babe?"

"I . . . *I want your legs wrapped around mine.* I hope you sleep well."

"You too, sweetie. Good night."

Good night, my darling, my love. I hold the pillow tightly against my body. A few tears run down my cheeks.

20

Drew has been cool toward me since the incident with Walter. When I see him waiting for me at my desk the morning after Manny and Peter and I visited the Reynosas, I dread his quiet, professional unfriendliness.

"Gloria, I need you to work the six-to-midnight shift tonight," he says.

"I can't tonight, Drew. I have a class."

"Cancel you class. I need you here tonight. I don't have a replacement for Manny's shift."

"What happened to the part-timer?"

"He was fired."

"Why did you fire him?"

"I didn't."

"Who could fire him?"

No answer.

"Who fired him, Drew?"

"Irma."

"Irma? Why, for heaven's sake?"

"I don't know. She just told me a few minutes ago. She wants you. She says you're good in that slot. Sorry. Please cancel your class, take over the shift. If you do it, I'll let you off the Children's Fair remote on Sunday. The whole staff is required to be there, but you can skip it, if you want." Darn Drew. He knows very well I won't skip the Children's Fair. I love it. I love to be surrounded by the little tykes, to blow up balloons for them and entertain them. I love to do funny voices and make them laugh. Drew knows I love it.

"Please do it," he says again. I'm feeling guilty that I caused Drew's confession concerning Walter, so I can't deny him his request.

"O.K., Drew. I'll take over." *And I won't see Peter. And I'll miss him!*

Manny's shift is a lonely shift. There's no one in the station. All the lights, except for those in the studio, are turned off. It's an eerie feeling knowing you're all alone in the entire building. Except for Mr. Jenkins.

Steve called a while ago to let me know the crazy fan is out on bond. To be especially careful. I'm hoping he doesn't call me. I'm uneasy enough as it is. I'm just playing music and chatting a bit with my listeners. No poems. No dedications. During one of the commercials I get up and walk to the front door to take a reassuring peek at Mr. Jenkins. With relief, I see that he's still is there. He smiles and gives a little wave. "Good show you have there, Miss Gloria," he calls out.

"Thank you, Mr. Jenkins. Would you like a cup of coffee?"

"No, thank's. I bring my sandwich and thermos here." He holds up a gray aluminum lunch box. The same kind I used to take to school.

"Got to hurry, Mr. Jenkins. The commercial is almost over." I dash back to my console.

The law class must be over. I hope Peter is listening to the radio and understands why I wasn't in class tonight. I hear the door to the studio opening slowly. I turn around.

"Oh, Irma. It's you. You gave me such a jolt. I didn't know anybody was here."

"Play 'I've Got you Under My Skin,'" she says. "It was Vincent's favorite. Play it now." She speaks softly. "It's my love song to him. My love song to my dear Vincent."

"Irma, it's not on the music list Drew gave me for tonight."

"Play it anyway. I want to hear it. I used to dance to it with Vincent. I miss him so." There's so much sadness in her voice, I'd like to go to her and comfort her. But I continue sitting in the deejay's chair, my earphones pulled down around my neck.

"Play it," she insists. It's a direct order. I get up and go to the CD rack on the far wall facing the door and pull out the CD with that song. I insert it and look at Irma. She's staring at me. Her look has changed completely. Her shoulders are thrown back, her eyes glistening, her mouth frozen in an ugly grimace.

"You know, don't you? You're the only one who does know." Her voice is very low, subdued. Her eyes are focused on me without blinking. She's standing in the middle of the studio with her hands stuck inside the pockets of her long gray skirt.

"You know. Don't deny it. You know I wasn't here the night Vince was killed. You imitated my voice. And you do such a good job that nobody would believe you that I wasn't here."

She walks toward me, getting closer as she speaks.

"Irma, what are you saying?"

"I know you've been poking around. Asking questions. Getting involved in everybody's affairs. I'm not going to let you destroy me. You hear that? I'm not going to let you." She pulls out a gun from her pocket and points it at me. A small silvery gun. I'm stunned but strangely, I also feel like laughing. It looks like a toy gun. A toy gun with a funny looking cylinder in front.

"Oh, my God." All of a sudden it all comes together."Of course, it was you. But why? He loved you so much. Was it because of Walter?"

"What? What are you talking about?" She looks genuinely startled.

"Because he discovered the affair you were having with Walter? I read your diary."

"My what? The diary?" Hysterical laughter. "You're an idiot. You know? An idiot! That was all made up. I did it for Vincent's pleasure. He liked to hear about my affairs with

other men. It turned him on. But when he read all the details
about my affair with Walter, he went crazy. Crazy for me.
Crazy with desire and anger and jealousy and violence. He
would beat me and bite me and scream at me. Afterwards, he
would go down on his knees and beg me to forgive him. I
would then lie down close to him and let him kiss me pas-
sionately, wildly. Those were the greatest moments of our
lovemaking. I would make up things in my diary and leave it
in different places where I knew he would find it. I don't
think he ever really knew whether I was with other men or
not. Part of our pleasure was for him to find out my secrets.
Or what he thought were my secrets. My affair with Walter,
the affair he thought I had with Walter, above all, drove him
crazy."

I'm dumbfounded. I just stare at Irma, not knowing what
to do. Her gun is pointed straight at me. "But why did you
kill him?" I manage to ask.

"Because I loved him. I wanted him and his children and
he wouldn't give me any. Because I was crazy with jealousy.
He cared about his other woman. And her baby. His baby and
hers. Because he was going to leave me and go live with his
bastard Donny, acknowledging him as his son, and leaving me
with nothing."

"Why did you set up Manny? What did he do to you?"

"He ignored me, that's what. And because it was so easy.
Manny, with his silly pride and his vain ways. He just could-
n't believe that someone could dislike him so much. And he
thought I invited him to the house out of lust." She laughs.
"Do you know that stupid man arrived at my house with a

bunch of roses? I was watching him and I nearly burst out laughing. Vain and stupid. Enough of this. Enough talk. You must go." She takes two more steps toward me, the gun inches away.

"Wait," I say to distract her while I move my hand slightly and turn on the switch so the voices in the studio are broadcast. "Don't do it."

"You know too much," she says. "And you believe in Manny. You can ruin me."

Oh God, please let somebody be listening. Let somebody realize this is not one of my crazy stunts or impersonations.

"But Irma, they'll know it was you who killed me." *My God is this real? Is she going to kill me?*

"No, they won't. I hid in my office all evening. No one knew I was here. The guard didn't see me come in. I'll use the back door to leave. Nobody will ever know I was here tonight. People will think it was your crazy fan who killed you. I knew he was calling you. Or did you think I didn't know? There's nothing, nothing at all that happens at this radio station that I don't know."

"You're forgetting. Mr. Jenkins will hear the gun go off."

"No, he won't. The gun has a silencer." She's relishing the moment, enjoying showing me how smart she is. "I have an old Manny tape prepared to run until the midnight deejay comes in. Your body won't be discovered until then. I have a great alibi prepared until then."

She cocks the gun and raises it to my temple. Suddenly the studio door bursts open. She whirls around, the gun pointed at Mr. Jenkins.

"Mrs. Halifax, please drop the gun," he says. "I'm going . . ."

I see her finger closing on the trigger. With all my force, I spring onto her back and take her down with me. She lands face down. I fall on top of her. I'm sure I'm crushing her face to the floor. I reach quickly for the fallen gun and grab it. Mr. Jenkins, big Mr. Jenkins, pounces on her. I hear her gasping for air. "I'm so sorry, Mrs. Halifax, I'm so sorry . . ." he keeps repeating.

My hand is shaking badly as I reach for the phone.

"Peter, are you there?"

"Yes, babe, I'm here. I missed you this evening."

"I need to see you, Peter. Right away. Will you please have a drink with me?"

"Where, babe?"

"Meet me at Max's Bar and Grill?"

"I'll be there in fifteen minutes."

"Peter?"

"Yes, babe?"

"I can't wait to see you."

"Me too, my sweet girl. Me too."

On my way to Max's I turn on the radio. It's one of Manny's old tapes:

"And for lovely Sara, 'with all my love' from Barry: 'You are my love and my life.' Beautifully said, Barry. Well put. Now let's hear this soulful song from the lovely Ms Celine Dion."

Manny's voice. My heart stirs. Such a beautiful, beautiful voice.